Edmund Kirke

Patriot Boys and, Prison Pictures

Edmund Kirke

Patriot Boys and, Prison Pictures

ISBN/EAN: 9783744757874

Printed in Europe, USA, Canada, Australia, Japan

Cover: Foto ©Andreas Hilbeck / pixelio.de

More available books at **www.hansebooks.com**

PATRIOT BOYS

AND

PRISON PICTURES.

PATRIOT BOYS

AND

PRISON PICTURES.

BY

EDMUND KIRKE,

AUTHOR OF "AMONG THE PINES," "MY SOUTHERN FRIENDS," ETC.

BOSTON:
TICKNOR AND FIELDS.
1866.

UNIVERSITY PRESS: WELCH, BIGELOW, & CO.,
CAMBRIDGE.

To

MASTER CHARLES BUCK BROOKS

THESE SKETCHES

ARE AFFECTIONATELY DEDICATED

BY

THE AUTHOR.

INTRODUCTION.

WE—"grandma," our young folks, and I—
live up here on the old battle-ground, in a
quaint, old-fashioned farm-house, older than many
of the old folks now living; and every day, when
the sun goes down, we gather round the great wood-
fire in the sitting-room, and talk and tell stories
by the hour together. I tell the most of the stories; for, though I am only a plain man, going
about in a slouched hat, a rusty coat, and a pair
of pantaloons old and threadbare enough to have
been worn by one of the Pilgrims, I have mingled
with men, seen a great many places, and been almost all over the world.

My own children like my stories, because they
think they are true, and because they are all about
the people I have met, and the places I have seen,

and so give them some glimpses of what is going on in the busy life outside of our quiet country home; but I do not expect other young folks to like them as well as my own do, — for their own father will not tell them. However, I have here written out a few of the many I know, in the hope that, if they are not as wonderful as the Arabian Nights, or as laughable as the Grimm Tales, they yet may afford some trifling pleasure and instruction to boys and girls I have never seen, and who gather of evenings around firesides far away from the one where all my stories are first told.

CONTENTS.

PATRIOT BOYS.

PRISON PICTURES.

LIST OF ILLUSTRATIONS.

———◆———

PATRIOT BOYS.

THE NEW HAMPSHIRE BOY.

ON the second and third days of May, 1863, was
fought the great and terrible battle of Chancellorville, and not until men beat their swords into
ploughshares, and boys exchange their drums for
jews-harps and penny-whistles, will it be forgotten.
But I do not propose to write about it, for I cannot.
No one can describe a battle without seeing it ; and
I did not see the battle of Chancellorville. But I
did see, more than a year after it was fought, a little
boy who was in it, and who, nearly all the interven-
ing time, was a prisoner in the hands of the Rebels.

He was only twelve years old, and you may think
that what such a little fellow did, at such a time,
could not be of much consequence to anybody. But
it was. He saved one or two human lives, and
lighted the passage of a score of souls through the
dark valley ; and so did more than any of our great
generals on those bloody days. He saved lives, —
they destroyed them.

You know that if you break a small wheel in a

cotton mill, the entire machinery will stop ; and if
the moon — one of the smallest lumps of matter in
the universe — should fall from its orbit, the whole
planetary system might go reeling and tumbling
about like a drunken man. So you see the great
importance of little things, — and little *folks* are of
much greater importance than little *things*. If they
were not, the little boy I am writing about would not
have done so much at Chancellorville, and I should
not now be telling you his story.

The battle was raging hotly on our left, when this
little drummer-boy was ordered to the rear by his
Captain. "Go," the Captain said; "you 're in danger here; back there you may be of use to the
wounded." The little fellow threw his musket over
his shoulder, — his drum he left behind when the
battle began, — and, amid the pelting bullets, made
his way back to the hospital. Our forces were driving the enemy, and all the ground over which they
had fought was strewn with the dead and the dying.
Here and there men with stretchers were going
about among the wounded; but the stretchers were
few, and the wounded were many; and as the poor
maimed and bleeding men turned their pitiful eyes
on the little boy, or in low, faint tones asked him for
water, he could not help lingering among them,

though the enemy's shells were bursting, and their bullets falling like hailstones all about him. Gray jackets were mingled with blue; but in a generous mind the cry of suffering dispels all distinction between friend and enemy; and Robert — that was his name — went alike to the wounded of both armies. Filling his canteen from a little stream which flowed through the battle-field, he held it to many a parched lip, and was rewarded with many a blessing from dying men, — blessings which will be to him a comfort and a consolation when he too shall draw near to death.

He had relieved a score or more, when he noticed, stretched on the ground at a little distance, his head resting against a tree, a fair-haired boy of not more than seventeen. He was neatly dressed in gray, and had a noble countenance, with a broad, open forehead, and thick, curly hair, which clustered all about his temples. His face wore the hue of health, his eyes were bright and sparkling, and only the position of his hands, which were clasped tightly above his head, told that he was in pain and wounded.

"Can I help you?" asked Robert, as he approached him.

"Thank you. Yes," he answered, clutching the canteen, and taking a long draught of the water.

B

"Thank you," he said again. "I saw you. I knew *you* would come to me."

"Why! have the rest passed you by?"

"Yes; for, you see, I'm a Rebel," he replied, smiling faintly. "But *you* don't care for that."

"No, I don't. But are you badly hurt?"

"Pretty badly, I fear. I'm bleeding fast, — I reckon it's all over with me"; — and he pointed to a dark red stain on his jacket, just under his shoulder. His voice had a clear, ringing tone, and his face a calm, cheerful look; for to the brave death has no terrors. To the true man or boy it is only the passage upward to a higher, better, nobler life in the heavens.

Robert tore open the young man's clothes, and bound his handkerchief tightly about his wound; then, seeing an empty stretcher coming that way, he shouted to its bearers: "Quick! Take him to the hospital. He's bleeding to death!"

"I don't like the color o' his clothes," said one of the men as the two moved on with the stretcher. "I guess he kin wait till we look arter our own wounded."

His face flushing with both shame and anger, Robert sprang to his feet, and, turning upon the men, said in an imperious tone, which sounded oddly enough from such a little fellow : " He can't wait. He will bleed to death, I tell you. Take him now ; if you don't, I 'll report you, — I 'll have you drummed out of the army for being brutes and cowards."

The men set down the litter, and the one who had spoken, looking pleasantly at Robert for a moment, said : " Well, you *are* a bully boy. We don't keer for no reportin' ; but for sich a little chap as you, we 'll do anything, — I 'm blamed if we won't."

" I thank you very much, said Robert, in an altered way, as he hastened to help the men lift the wounded youth upon the stretcher.

The hospital was an old mill at a cross-roads, about a quarter of a mile away. It was built of logs, without doors or window-panes, and was fast falling to decay ; but its floor, and nearly every square inch of shaded ground around it, were covered with the wounded and the dying. Thither they bore the Rebel boy, and, picking their way among the many prostrate and bleeding men, spread a blanket under a tree, and laid him gently on it. Then Robert went for a surgeon.

One shortly came, and, after dressing the wound, he said in a kindly way : " It 's a bad hurt, my lad, but keep up a good heart, and you 'll soon be about.

A little pluck does more for a wound than a good
many bandages."

"Oh! Now you 've stopped the bleeding, I
sha'nt die. I *won't* die, — it would kill mother if
I did."

And so, you see, the Southern lad, even then,
thought of his mother! and so do all brave boys,
whether well or wounded. They think of her first,
and of her last; for no other hand is so tender, no
other voice is so gentle, no other heart so true and
faithful as hers. No boy ever grew to be a great
and good man, who did not love and reverence his
mother. Even the Saviour of the world, when he
hung upon the cross, thought of his, and said to
John, "Behold thy mother!"

With so many needing help, Robert could do
little more for the Southern youth. He saw him
covered warmly with a blanket, and heard him say,
"Whether I get well or not, I shall never forget
you." Then he left him, not to see him again till
long afterwards.

The surgeon was a kind-hearted man, and told
Robert he should not go again upon the battle-
ground; so he went about among the wounded in
the hospital, tending them, writing last words to
their loved ones at home, or reading to them from

the blessed Book which God has given to be the
guide of the living and the comfort of the dying.

So the day wore away, until the red tide of battle
surged again around the old mill at the cross-roads.
The Rebels came on in overpowering force, and
drove our men, as autumn leaves are driven before
the whirlwind. Numbers went down at every volley; and right there, not a hundred yards away, a
tall, stalwart man fell, mortally wounded. A Rebel
bullet had entered his side, and as the fallen man
pressed his hand upon it, a dog which was with him
began to lap the wound, as if he thought he could
thus stay the crimson stream on which his master's
soul was going to its Maker.

Robert saw the man fall, and the dog standing by
amid the leaden storm which was pouring in torrents all around them. Admiring the bravery of
the dog, he stepped out from behind the tree where
he had stood out of range of the bullets, and went
to the wounded man. Gently lifting his head, he
said to him, "Can I do anything for you?"

"Yes!" gasped the man. "Tell them that I died
—like a man—for my country."

"Is that all? Nothing more?" asked Robert
quickly, for he saw that the soldier was sinking rapidly.

The dying man turned his eyes to the boy's face, clasped his arm tightly about the neck of his dog, made one or two efforts to speak, and then, murmuring faintly, "Take care — of — Ponto!" passed to that world where are no wars and no fightings.

The battle by this time had surged away to the northward, and a small party of cavalry-men had halted before the doorway of the hospital. Robert had closed the eyes of the fallen soldier, and was straightening his limbs on the blood-dampened ground, when one of the horsemen called out to him: "What, — my little fellow! What are you doing out here, — so far away from your mother?"

Robert looked up, and, amid the group of officers, saw a tall, broad-shouldered, grave-looking man, with handsome, regular features, and hair and beard streaked with gray, but almost as white as cotton. He wore a high felt hat, an old gray coat, and blue trousers tucked into high top-boots; and he rode a large, handsome horse, whose skin was as soft and glossy as a leopard's. He carried no arms, but the three dingy stars on his collar showed that he held high rank among the Rebels. All this Robert had time to observe as he very deliberately answered: "I came out here, sir, to help fight the wicked men who are trying to destroy their country."

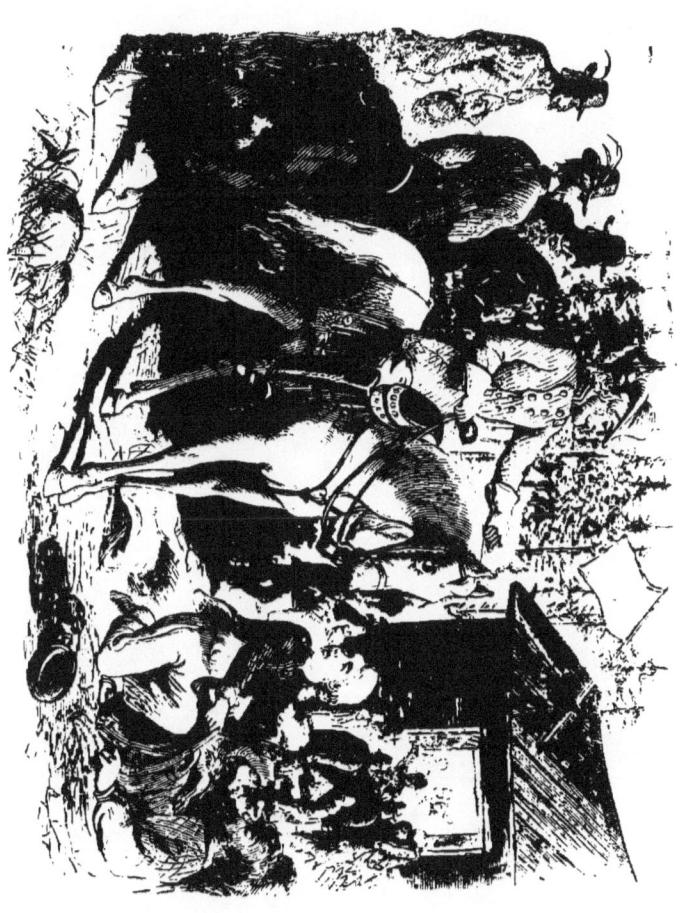

The officer's placid face flushed with anger; and, turning to an aid, he said, in a harsh, grating tone: "Take that boy to the rear. Send him to the Libby with the other prisoners."*

Robert did not then know that this officer was the famous General Lee, — the man who neither smokes, drinks, nor chews tobacco; who has, in short, none of the smaller vices, but all of the larger ones; for he deliberately, basely, and under circumstances of unparalleled meanness, betrayed his country, and, long after all hope of success was lost, carried on a murderous war against his own race and kindred.

It was nearly sunset before Robert was sent off to the rear, and meanwhile a narrow trench was scooped in the ground, and the dead soldier was placed in it. Robert set a small stake at the head of the grave, and it stands there still; but no one knows who rests below, and no one will know till the morning of the resurrection; and yet it may be that even now, in some far-away Northern home, hearts are heavy, and eyes are red, with waiting and weeping for the father and the husband who never again will return to his loved among the living.

* This incident is corroborated to the writer by a lady to whom it was related by Lieutenant-Colonel Botts, — nephew to Hon. John Minor Botts, — who was a member of Lee's staff, and present when it occurred.

Early on the following day, with about three hundred poor fellows, one half of whom were wounded, Robert was marched off to Richmond. The soldier's dog, when he saw his master laid away in the ground, howled and took on piteously, but soon afterwards grew friendly with Robert, and the two made all the weary journey together.

It was in truth a weary journey, and I cannot find it in my heart to tell you about it, for I do not want to make you sad; and it would draw tears from hearts of stone to know all that the poor boy endured. It seemed more than human nature could bear, and yet it was only what thousands of our tired, footsore, wounded, and starving men have suffered on their long, dusty, and muddy march to the Richmond Bastile. Time and again the little boy would have fallen by the way, had not the poor dumb dog sustained him. They shared their meagre crust together; and often, when Robert's spirits drooped on the march, Ponto would gambol about him, and make him cheerful in spite of himself; and often, too, when he lay down to sleep on the damp ground, the dog would stretch his huge paws across his breast, and cover him, as well as he could, from the cold air and the unhealthy night dew.

At sunset, on the fourteenth day of May, the column, wayworn and footsore, with haggard faces and uncombed hair, was set down from the cars of the Virginia Central Railroad, and marched into the city of Richmond. Down the long, grass-grown streets they were hurried, with clouded faces and heavy hearts ; but when at last the cold, brown walls of the Libby rose before them darkly outlined on the gray sky, they almost shouted for joy, — for joy that their toilsome journey was over, though it had ended in a prison. If they had known of the many weary months of cold and hunger and misery which some of them were to pass there, would they not rather have died than have entered the dark doorway of that living grave?

All of you have read descriptions, or seen pictures, of the gloomy outside of this famous prison, so I need not tell you how it looks. It is indeed gloomy, but the inside is repulsive and unsightly to the last degree. The room into which Robert and his companions were taken was a long, low apartment on the ground floor, with naked beams, broken windows, in whose battered frames the spider had woven his web, and bare brown walls, from which hung scores of torn, dingy blankets, every one of them filled with a larger caravan of wild animals than any ever seen in a Northern town. The weary,

2

travel-soiled company was soon ranged in four files along the floor of this room, and there they were made to wait two long hours for the Inspector. At last he came, — a coarse, brutal fellow, with breath perfumed with whiskey, and face bloated with drink and smeared with tobacco-juice.

"Yer a' sorry set!" he said, as he went down the lines, taking from the men their money and other valuables. "A sorry set!" he added, as he looked down on their ragged clothes, through which here and there the torn flesh was peeping. "A sorry set! Sorrier nur purtater-tops in September; but yer green though, — greener nur laurel-bushes, and ye bar [bear] better," again he said, as he stuffed a huge handful of United States notes into his pocket, and went on with his dirty work. At last he stopped before a coatless officer, with matted hair, only one boot, a tattered shirt, and no hat or neck-tie, but in their stead a stained bandage, from under which the blood still was trickling. "Who'd ha' thought o' raisin' sich a crap from sich a hill o' beans!" he said, as he drew from the pocket of this officer a roll larger than usual, and in his greed paused to count the money.

"We reap what we sow," said the officer, with a look of intense loathing; "you are sowing theft, you'll reap hell-fire, — if I live to get out of this prison."

"Yer sowin' greenbacks, and ye'll reap a dungeon, if ye don't keep a civil tongue in yer head," responded the fellow, with a brutal sneer, as he went on down the column.

Ponto had kept close to the heels of Robert, and, following him into the prison, had crouched down behind the line, and remained unobserved until the robbery was over. Then a dozen sentinels were ordered to take the prisoners to their quarters, and, when they began to move, the dog attracted the notice of the Inspector. "Whose dog is that?" he roared, as Ponto started up the stairway, a little in advance of his young master.

Robert was about to answer, but a kind-hearted sentinel, seeing from his looks that the dog was his, touched him on the shoulder, and whispered : "Not a word, Sonny! It mout git ye inter trouble."

"Stop him! Cotch that dog!" shouted the Inspector, as Ponto, hearing the inquiry, and seeming to know by instinct that it referred to him, darted forward and disappeared in the room above. The Inspector and two or three sentries pursued him, and, bounding after them two steps at a time, Robert soon saw what followed.

The room was of the same size, and furnished in much the same way, as the one below stairs; but scattered about it, in messes of fifteen or twenty, were more than two hundred prisoners. In and out among these prisoners ran the dog and his pursuers. It was an exciting chase; but they might as well have tried to catch a sunbeam, or a bird without salting its tail, as to take Ponto in such a crowd of friends. In and out among them — crouching behind boxes, leaping over barrels, running beneath benches, right under the legs of his pursuers — went Ponto, as if he were a streak of lightning out on a frolic; while the prisoners stood by, laughing, and shouting, and getting in the way as much as possible, to keep the loyal dog from the clutches of his Rebel enemies. Half an hour the chase lasted. Then the patience of the Inspector gave out, and, puffing with heat and anger, he shouted, "One of you, shoot the —— critter."

A sentinel levelled his musket, but a Union man threw up the barrel. "Don't fire here," he said, "you 'll kill some of us."

"Fire, —— you, fire! Don't mind him," shouted the enraged Inspector.

"Do it, Dick Turner," said the man, planting himself squarely before him, "and I 'll brain you on the

spot," and — Turner prudently omitted to order the
shooting.

Taking advantage of this momentary lull, Ponto
darted up into the officer's room, and was soon snugly hid away in the third story. Baffled and exasper-
ated, Turner turned to the man, and growling out,
"I'll have my revenge for this, my fine fellow,"
strode down the stairway.

Robert's quarters were in the room where this
scene occurred, and his new messmates received him
very kindly. They gave him food, bathed his aching,
swollen limbs, and soon made him a bed on the floor,
with a blanket for a mattress, and Ponto for a cover-
let. He was just falling into a doze, when he heard
a voice at the landing ask, with an oath, "Where is
that dog?" The lights were out, but by the lantern
which the man carried, the boy saw that he was a
short, slight, dapper individual, with a beardless face,
a sneaking look, and a consequential air, which seemed
to say: "Get out of my way, sir; I am Thomas P.
Turner, professional Negro-whipper, but now keeper
of Libby Prison, and I take off my hat to nobody."
With him was the other Turner, — his tool, and the
fit instrument of his contemptible tyranny.

No one answered the question, and the two worthies groped their way about the room with the lan-

tern. They caught sight of Robert's mess just in time to see Ponto again take himself off up the stairway. The sagacious creature had heard the ungentlemanly allusion to himself, and, like a sensible dog, determined to keep out of such low company.

With the aid of his Union friends, that night and for a week afterwards, Ponto baffled his pursuers; but at last he was taken, and, much against his will, was set free — for, you know, it is only men that ever deserve to be shut up in prison. What became of him Robert does not know; but if he is living, he is a decent dog; if dead, he has gone where the good dogs go, — that is certain.

"So, he is your dog?" said Turner, halting before Robert, who had risen to his feet.

"He is, sir," answered the little boy in a respectful tone, "and you will be cruel if you take him away from me."

"Cruel! do you call *me* cruel!" cried Turner, flying into a passion. "I 'll teach you manners, you young whelp." Turning then to his subordinate, he asked for the "other Yankee."

The prisoner who had forbidden the firing was pointed out, and soon he and Robert were escorted to a dungeon, down in the cellar, under the sidewalk. The members of Robert's mess told Turner of his exhausted condition, and begged him not to consign a tired, sick boy to so horrible a place, — at least to let him rest where he was till the morning; but all they said was of no avail. They might as well have talked to an adder, for an adder is not more deaf, nor more venomous, than was that man!

So Robert's long, weary journey ended in a dungeon. It was a horrid den, — a low, close, dismal place, with a floor encrusted with filth, and walls stained and damp with the rain, which in wet weather had dripped down from the sidewalk. Its every corner was alive with vermin, and it seemed only a fit habitation for some ferocious beast, which had to be shut out from the light of day, and kept from contact with all things human. Yet into it they thrust a sick, fragile boy; and he would have died there but for the kind-hearted soldier who went with him. He wrapped him in his blanket; gave him every morsel of his own food; stretched himself on the naked floor, and held him for hours clasped to his own warm breast; and, in all ways, nursed and tended him as if he had been his mother. So Robert lived through it, and, at the end of forty hours, God softened the hearts of his keepers.*

* This whole narrative of Robert's stay in the Libby the writer has on the testimony of two persons besides the boy

For a month afterwards Robert was confined to the hospital. The occupant of the next cot to his own was a Union Colonel, who, when they were well enough to go back to the prison, procured for him admission to the officers' quarters in the third story. This secured him no better fare or accommodations than he would have had below with the private soldiers, but it gave him more air and larger space to move about in. There he lived for seven long months; sleeping, at night, on the hard floor; idling, by day, through the large rooms, or gazing out on the narrow prospect to be seen from the prison windows. But his time was not altogether idled away. Under the eye of the good Colonel, he went over his arithmetic and grammar, and learned French and Spanish. But it was a weary time. Exchanges were suspended, and there seemed no hope; yet at last deliverance came.

Robert went seldom from his own floor, but one cold day in January, 1864, he was called by a simple errand to the lower story. He was about returning, his foot was even on the stairway, when he heard some one call his name. Looking round, he saw it

himself. It is undoubtedly true in every detail. The writer would be convinced of it from what he personally knows of the two Turners, had he no other evidence.

was the sentinel, — a young man, with light, wavy hair, and an open, handsome countenance. His left coat-sleeve was dangling at his side, but he seemed strong, and otherwise capable of military duty. "Did you call me?" asked Robert. "Why!" cried the other, grasping his hand, "don't you know me? don't you remember Chancellorville?" It was the Rebel youth whose life Robert had saved on the battle-field. The musket dropped from his hand, and he hugged the little boy as if he had been his own brother. The other sentries, and even an officer stood by, and said nothing; though all this was against the prison regulations. After all, — after even the atrocities the Rebels have committed, — it is true that the same humanity beats under a gray coat that beats under a blue one.

The next day a gentleman came into the room where Robert was quartered, and asked to see him. He was a stoutly built man, rather above the medium height, with a full, open face, large pleasant eyes, and an agreeable manner. He was dressed in dark-gray clothes, wore a broad felt hat, and everything about him seemed to denote that he was a kind-hearted gentleman. He asked Robert how old he was; where his home was; how long he had been in prison; and all about his mother; and, when he rose to go away, gave him his hand, and said: "You're a brave boy. I am sorry I have n't known of you before. But you shall go home now, — in a few days I shall be going to the lines, and will take you with me.

Robert's eyes filled with tears, and he stammered out: "I thank you, sir. I thank you very much, sir."

"You need not, my boy," said the gentleman, placing his hand kindly upon his head. "It is only right that we should let you go, — you saved the life of one of our men."

In three days, with money in his pocket, given him by this gentleman, Robert was on his way to his mother. He is now at his home, fitting himself to act his part in this great world, in this earnest time in which we are living; and the kind-hearted man who set him free, charged with dishonest meanness and theft, is now shut up in that same horrid prison. Robert does not think him guilty, and he has asked me to tell you this about him, which I do gladly, and all the more gladly because I know him, and believe that, if there is an honorable, high-minded man in all Virginia, that man is ROBERT OULD.*

* Since this was written, Judge Ould has been honorably acquitted of all the charges against him.

THE ILLINOIS BOY.

ONE bleak day in October, 1853, a little boy
was playing with his dog on the floor of his
father's library, in one of the larger towns of Western Illinois. The dog was not bigger than a piece
of chalk; but when the boy ranged the great divin-
ity books into a railway-train along the floor, he
hopped upon them, and puffed and snorted away, as
if he supposed himself some huge engine racing
across the country under a full head of steam. "Whiz!
whiz!" and "Puff! puff!" went the dog, and "Hurrah! hurrah!" "Clear the track!" "Look out for
the bullgine!" shouted the boy, until the room shook,
and the dusty old worthies on the shelves crawled,
trembling, into their nightcaps, frightened out of
their few wits by this new development of the nine-
teenth century. How the tall man writing at the
desk managed to put two ideas together amid such
a din, I never could understand, until my own "Billy
Boy" had turned my own library into a railroad-
station.

At last the tall man laid down his pen, and, reaching up for his hat, which hung against the wall, caught sight of the boy, the dog, and the "Great Western Railway." Bursting into a merry laugh, he said : —

> "Willie had a little dog,
>   Whose coat was white as snow ;
>   And everywhere that Willie went
>   The dog was sure to go."

The boy sprang to his feet, and, catching up his own little hat, which lay on a chair in the corner, shouted out : —

> "And father had a little boy,
>   Whose face was white as snow ;
>   And everywhere that father went
>   The boy was sure to go."

In vain the father said that four-year-old boys should stay at home in stormy weather ; the little fellow insisted on going out, and finally carried his point ; and always afterwards, "everywhere the father went, the boy was sure to go."

So it came about that, one day in the following summer, when his father went a-shooting, Willie thrust the powder-horn into his pocket, and trudged off upon the prairie with him. They soon started a flock of quails, and Willie's father raised his gun

to fire among them; but, the little boy being very
near, he hesitated to shoot, lest he should frighten
him with the report of the weapon. Willie, seeing
the quails flying away, and the gun so strangely
hanging fire, cried out, impatiently, "Father, shoot!
Why don't you shoot?" But the father still hesitated; and then the boy, who knew nothing of a
gun but that it makes a loud noise, and is a dangerous thing to handle, cried out again: "Why, father,
are you afraid? Give *me* the gun, I'll shoot."

The father rested the gun across a log, and the
boy fired at the flock of quails. The birds had
flown beyond range, and the shot only hit the empty
air; but the little boy turned to his father, and said,
in a tone of cool and refreshing dignity, "There, father, don't you see there isn't any danger in firing
a gun!"

It was about this time that Willie went to his first
camp-meeting. Many of you have been at camp-
meetings, and know that they are religious gatherings, held in the open air, and attended by great
numbers of people, who go into the woods to wor-
ship, and frequently stay there days and weeks together. Willie's father was the president of a college; but he also was a clergyman, — and a clergyman who never omitted an opportunity of bearing

"testimony to the truth," whether in a church, a lecture-room, or at a camp-meeting. So it happened that on the occasion I speak of he was asked to occupy a place on the platform, and Willie took a seat beside him.

Another clergyman opened the meeting with prayer; but the prayer had scarcely begun, when one of the congregation — an ill-mannered mule, tethered near by in the timber — set up a most discordant braying, which drowned the voice of the speaker, and greatly disconcerted the worshippers. All at once the prayer ceased, and Willie's father, rising, asked that the mule might be led out of hearing. "Why, father," then exclaimed the little boy, "I thought you went for freedom of speech!"

"The boy is father of the man," and the small boy is father of the larger boy. This is shown by these little stories, which display traits in Willie's character that made him, long afterwards, put on a blue jacket and trousers, and follow his brave father over nearly every battle-field of the Southwest. He loved his father, and wanted to be always with him; he was not afraid of powder, or a shot-gun; and he went, to the full extent, for freedom of speech, — the principle which, though it may not do for asses and mules, lies at the very foundation of human liberty. So, when the South aimed a death-blow at this principle, and his father went out to uphold it on the battle-field, it was only natural that Willie should want to go with him, and have another shot at a flock of birds, — though these "birds" were not of the quail species.

His father had been in the army more than a year, and had risen to the command of a regiment, before he consented to take Willie along with him as a drummer-boy. Then he went, but had been at the front only a week when the army came in presence of the enemy, and was drawn up in two long lines to wait an attack. When an army is moving, drummer-boys and other musicians march at the head of their regiments ; but when it goes into battle, they are sent to the rear, to care for the wounded. On this occasion, however, when Willie's father rode along the lines, encouraging the soldiers to act like men in the coming conflict, he caught sight of the little drummer-boy, standing, with his drum over his shoulder, at the very head of the column.

"We are going into the fight, my son," said the father. "Your place is at the rear."

"Father," answered the boy, "if I go back there, everybody'll say I am a coward."

"Well, well," said his father, "stay where you are!"

He stayed there, and, when the attack began, moved in at the head of his regiment; and though the bullets hissed, the canister rattled, and the shells burst all about him, he came out uninjured. In the midst of the fight, when our men were going down before the storm of lead, as blades of grass go down before a storm of hail, one of the regimental orderlies was swept from his saddle by a cannon-ball, and his horse went galloping madly over the battle-field. Willie saw the orderly fall, and his horse bound swiftly away; and, leaving the ranks, he caught the frightened animal, and sprang into the fallen man's saddle. Riding then up to his father, he said: "Father, I'm tired of drumming, — I'd rather carry your orders."

He was only thirteen years old; but after that, in all the great battles of the Southwest, he acted as orderly for the brave Colonel, carrying his messages through the fiery storm, and riding unharmed up to the very cannon's mouth, until he was taken prisoner by the Rebels on the bloody field of Chickamauga.

All day long on that terrible Saturday he rode through the fight by the side of his father, and at night lay down on the ground to dream of his home and his mother. The battle paused when the sun went down; but soon after it had risen, on the fol-

lowing day, red and ghastly in the smoky air, the
faint crack of musketry and the heavy roar of artillery, sounding miles away, told that the brave
boys on our left were meeting the desperate onsets
of the enemy. Fiercely the Rebels broke against
their ranks, fiercely as the storm-wave breaks on a
rock in the ocean ; but like a rock, the brave Thomas
and his men beat back the wild surges, till they
rolled away in broken waves upon our centre and
right, where the little boy was with his regiment.
Battle and disease had thinned their ranks, and then
they numbered scarcely four hundred : but bravely
they stood up to meet the wild shock that was coming. Soon the Colonel's horse went down, and,
giving him his own, Willie hurried to the rear for
another. He had scarcely rejoined the ranks, when
on they came, — the fierce rangers of Texas and
Arkansas, — riding over the brigades of Davis and
Van Cleve, and the division of the gallant Sheridan,
as if they were only standing wheat all ripe for mowing. One half of the brave Illinois boys were on
the ground, wounded or dying ; but the rest stood
up, unmoved in the fiery hurricane which was sweeping in fierce gusts around them. Such men can die,
but their legs are not fashioned for running. Soon
both their flanks were enveloped in flame, and a

dreadful volley burst out of the smoke, and again the brave Colonel went to the ground in the midst of his heroes. Then the boy sprang to his side.

"Are you dead, father, or only wounded?"

"Neither, my boy," answered the iron man, as he clutched the bridle of a riderless horse, and sprang into the empty saddle. Two horses had been shot under him, and two hundred of his men had gone down forever, but still he sat there unmoved amid the terrible tempest. At last the fire grew even hotter; one unbroken sheet of flame enveloped the little band, and step by step, with their faces to the foe, they were swept back by the mere force of numbers. Then the father said to the boy, "Go, my son, to the rear, fast as your horse's legs can carry you."

"I can't, father," answered the lad, "you may be wounded."

"Never mind me; think of your mother. Go," said the father, peremptorily.

Obedience had been the rule of the boy's life. He said no more; but, turning his horse's head, rode back to the hospital.*

* This incident is thus related by an eyewitness of the battle, writing from the field on that terrible Sunday : — "Beside Colonel ———, of the Seventy-third Illinois, rode his son,

The hospital was a few tents clustered among the trees, a short distance in the rear ; and thither our wounded men were being conveyed as fast as the few medical attendants could carry them. There the boy dismounted, and set about doing all he could for the sufferers. While thus engaged, he saw his father's regiment emerge from the cloud of flame, and fall slowly back towards a wood behind them. In a moment a horde of rangers, uttering fierce yells, poured down on their flanks to envelop the little band of heroes. The boy looked, and at a glance took in his own danger. The hospital would inevitably be surrounded, and all in it captured ! He had heard of the Libby, and the prison-pens of Salisbury and Andersonville ; and springing upon the back of the nearest horse, he put spurs to its sides and bounded away towards the forest. But it was a clumsy beast, not the blooded animal which

a lad of thirteen ; a bright, brave little fellow, who believed in his father, and feared nothing. Right up to the enemy, — right up anywhere, — if the father went, there went the boy ; but when the bullets swept in sheets, and grape and canister cut ragged roads through the columns of blue, and plashed them with red, the father bade the young orderly out of the fiery gust. The little fellow wheeled his horse and rode for the hospital. The hospital was captured, and the boy a prisoner." — B. F. TAYLOR, in *Chicago Journal.*

had borne him so nobly through the day's conflict. Slowly it trotted along, though the rowels pierced its flanks till the blood ran down them in a rivulet. The forest was yet a long way off when the rangers caught sight of the boy and the sleepy animal, and gave chase, brandishing their carbines and yelling like a regiment of demons. The boy heard the shouts, and slung himself along the side of his horse to be out of range of bullets; but not one of the rangers offered to fire, or even lifted his carbine; for there is something in the breasts of these half-savage men that makes them in love with daring; and this running with a score of rifles following at one's heels is about as dangerous as a steeple-chase over a country filled with pitfalls and torpedoes.

Soon the rangers' fleet steeds encircled the boy's clumsy animal, and one of them seized his bridle, crying out, "Yer a bully 'un; jest the pluckiest chunk uv a boy I uver seed."

Willie was now a prisoner, and prudence counselled him to make the best of a bad business; so he slid nimbly to the ground, and coolly answered, "Give me a hundred yards the start, and I'll get away yet, — if my horse *is* slower than a turtle."

"I'm durned ef we won't," shouted the man. "I say, fellers, guv the boy forty rod, and let him go scot free ef he gits fust ter the timber."

".None uv yer nonsense, Tom," said another, who seemed some petty officer. " Luck at the boy's cloes? He 's son ter some o' the big 'uns. I 'll bet high he b'longs ter ole Linkum hisself. I say, young 'un, hain't ye ole Linkum's boy?"

" I reckon!" answered Willie, laughing, in spite of his unpleasant surroundings.

But what he said in jest was received in earnest; and with a suppressed chuckle the man said: "I knowed it. Fellers, he 's good fur a hundred thousand, — so let 's keep a bright eye on him."

Willie was a boy of truth. He had been taught to value his word above everything, even life; but the men were deceiving themselves, and he was not bound to undeceive them to his own disadvantage. He had heard of the barbarity they had shown to helpless prisoners, and his keen mother wit told him to be silent, for this false impression would insure him kind and respectful treatment. After a short consultation, the rangers told him to mount his horse again, and then led him by a circuitous route, to be out of range of the fire of our retreating forces, to a hospital a short distance in the rear of the Rebel lines, where a large number of prisoners were gathered. On the way one of them asked Willie the time of day, and, when he drew out his watch, coolly took it and placed it in his pocket; but they offered him no other wrong or indignity.

Arrived at the station, the leader of the rangers rode up to the officer in charge of the prisoners, and said : "I say, Cunnel, we 'se cotched a fish yere as is wuth cotchin', — one o' ole Linkum's boys !"

The officer scrutinized Willie closely, and then said, "Are you President Lincoln's son ?"

"No, sir," answered Willie; "but I am 'one of Linkum's boys.'"

· "Ye telled me ye war, ye young hound !" cried the ranger, breaking into a storm of oaths and curses.

"I did not," said Willie coolly; "I let you deceive yourself, — that was all."

The rangers stormed away as if they were a dozen hurricanes exercising their lungs for an evening concert; but the Colonel, who at first had gone into an uncontrollable fit of laughter, now turned upon them with a torrent of reproaches. "You 're a set of cowards," he said. "You have got this up to get away from the fight. A dozen of you to guard a twelve-year-old boy ! Begone ! Back to the lines every one of you, or I 'll report you. Old Bragg has a way of dealing with skulkers such as you are."

The rangers needed no further hint. They galloped off, and Willie walked away and joined the other prisoners.

About a thousand of our tired and wounded men, under guard of two companies of Rebel soldiers, were collected in an open field not far from the hospital; and with them, without food, without shelter, and with nothing but the hard ground to lie on, the little boy remained till noon of the following day.

At night he lay down to rest in a crotch of the fence and counted the stars, as one by one they came out in the sky, telling of the Great All-Father who has his home in the high heavens, but comes down to visit and relieve his heart-weary children who are wandering here on the earth. Was *he* not heart-weary, — heart-weary with thinking of his home and his mother, who soon would be sorrowing for her only son, lost amid the wild storm of battle? And would not God visit and relieve *him?* As he thought of this, he prayed. Rising to his knees, he said the little prayer he had said every morning and evening since his earliest childhood; and even as he prayed, a dark cloud broke away over his head, and the north star came out and looked down, as if sent by the good Father to guide him homeward.

He watched the star growing brighter and brighter, till its gentle rays stole into his soul, lighting all its dark corners; and then he sunk to sleep and dreamed, — dreamed that a white-robed angel came and took him in its arms and bore him away, above the tree-tops, to his father's tent beyond the mountains. His father was on his knees praying; and while he prayed the angel vanished, and in its place came the spirits of his ancestors, — the hunted Huguenots, who had gone up to Heaven from many a blood-sodden battle-field. They took the boy by the hand and said, "Be strong, and fear not. Put your trust in God, and he will show you a safe way out of the wilderness."

In the morning he woke hopeful and stout-hearted. Kneeling down, he prayed again; and then a plan of escape came to him, — clear and distinct as ever plan of battle came to a general. He did not think it out; it came to him like a beam of light breaking into a dark room; or like a world-stirring thought flashing into the soul of genius from the Source of all thought in the heavens. But this thought was not to stir a world; it was only to stir a small boy's legs, and make him a man in resource and resolution. Long he pondered upon it, turning it round and round, and looking at it from all sides; and then he set about working it out into action.

The Colonel commanding the guard was a mild-

mannered man, with pleasant features, and a heart
evidently too good to be engaged in the wicked
work of rebellion. Him the boy accosted as he
made his morning round among the prisoners. "You
seem to be short-handed at the hospital, sir," he
said; "I have done such work, and would be glad
to be of service."

"You're a good boy to think of it," replied the
officer, — "too good to be one of Lincoln's boys,"
— and he laughed heartily at the recollection. "But
won't you try to get away if I let you go there?"

"I can't promise," said Willie; "you would n't if
you were a prisoner."

"No, I would n't," answered the Colonel, kindly.
"But it won't be safe for you to try. Some of our
men are wild fellows, and they would shoot you
down as soon as they would a squirrel. The Union
lines are twelve miles away, and our pickets are
thicker than the fleas in this cornfield."

"I 'd rather not be shot, — I 'd rather be a prisoner," said Willie, smiling.

"You're a sensible lad," answered the officer,
laughing. "I 'll let you into the hospital, and you
may get away if you can; but if you are shot, don't
come back and say I did it."

"I don't believe in ghosts," said the little boy,

3   D

following the Colonel on his rounds, to be sure he should not forget him.

When the officer's duties were over, he took, Willie from the cornfield and gave him in charge to Doctor Hurburt, chief surgeon of the hospital. The doctor was a humane, kind-hearted man, and he laughed heartily at the story of the boy's capture by the rangers. "You served them right, my little fellow," he said, "and you are smart, — smart enough to be a surgeon. There is plenty to do here, and if you go to work with a will, I 'll say a good word for you."

And the kind surgeon did ; and Willie's father afterwards bore him his thanks across many leagues of hostile country.

The hospital was a little village of tents, scattered about among the trees, and in it were nearly a thousand Rebel and Union soldiers, all of them either wounded or dying. Among them Willie worked for a fortnight. He scraped lint for their wounds, bound bandages about their limbs, held water to their parched lips, wrote last words to their far-away friends, and spoke peace to their souls as, weary and sin-laden, they groped their way through the dark valley that leads to the realm of the departed.

Among the patients was one in whom Willie took especial interest, — a bright-eyed, fair-haired boy, not

far from his own age, who had been wounded in the
great battle. He was a Rebel boy, but he had gone
into the war with the same purpose as Willie, — to
do all he could for what he thought was freedom.
He had been told that the North wanted to enslave
the South, and his soul rose in a strong resolve to
give his young life, if need be, to beat back his country's invaders. In all this he was wrong ; but only
a demagogue will say that the spirit which moved
him was not as noble as that which has led many a
Northern lad to be a martyr for real liberty. Young
as he was, he had been in half a dozen battles, and
in the bloody struggle of Chickamauga had fallen
pierced with two Union bullets. For two days and
nights he lay on the battle-field before he was discovered by the party of men who brought him to
the hospital. Willie helped to bear him from the
ambulance, and to lay him on a blanket in one of
the tents, and then went for the chief surgeon. A
bullet had entered the boy's side, and another crushed
the bones of his ankle. His leg had to come off,
and the amputation, the long exposure, and the loss
of blood, rendered his recovery almost hopeless.
The kind-hearted surgeon said this to Willie, as he
finished the operation, and bade him tell it to the
Rebel lad as gently as was possible. Willie did

this, and then the wounded boy, turning his mild gray eye to Willie's face, said calmly: "I thank you, —but for two days I have been expecting it. I have a pleasant home, a dear mother, and a kind little sister, and it is hard to leave them; but I am willing to go, for God has other work for me — up there — where the good angels are working."

He lingered for a week, every day growing weaker and weaker, and then sunk to sleep as gently as the water-drop sinks into the depths of the ocean. A few hours before he died he sent for Willie, and said to him: "You have been very good to me, and I would, as far as I can, return your kindness. My clothes are under my pillow. Take them when I am gone. They may help you to get back to your mother. I am going soon. Be with me when I die."

They laid him away in the ground, and Willie went about his work; but something loving and pure had gone out of his life, leaving him lone and heart-weary. He did not know that the little acts of kindness he had done to the dying boy would be reflected back in his own heart, and throw a gentle radiance round his life forever.

I would like to tell you all the details of Willie's escape, — how he dressed himself in the Rebel boy's clothes, and one cloudy night boldly passed the sentinels at the hospital; how he fell in with several squads of Rebel soldiers, was questioned by them, and safely got away because of his gray uniform; how, on his hands and knees, he crept beyond the Rebel pickets, and, after wandering in the woods two days and nights, with only the sun by day and the north star by night to guide him, got within our lines, and, exhausted from want of food and worn out with walking, lay down under a tree by the roadside, and slept soundly till the following night approached. I would like to tell you of all this, but if I did there would not be room for the other stories. So I will only say that Willie was roused from his slumbers under the tree by some one shaking him by the shoulder, and, looking up, saw a small party of Union cavalry.

"What are you doing here, my young grayback?" said the orderly, who had awakened him.

Willie was about to answer, when he caught sight of a face that was familiar. It was that of his mother's own brother, Colonel McIntyre, of the Forty-second Regiment of Indiana Infantry. The boy sprang to his feet and called out, "Why, uncle! don't you know me, — Willie ——?" In a moment he was on the back of the Colonel's horse, and on the way to his father.

But what of the boy's father, while his only son was a prisoner with the Rebels, or wandering thus alone in the wilderness?

I have told you that slowly and steadily the brave Colonel moved the remnant of his regiment out of the fiery storm on that terrible Sunday. At dusk of that day, he threw his men into bivouac at Rossville, miles away from the scene of conflict. There he learned that the regimental hospital had been captured, and Willie flung out alone — a little waif — on the turbulent sea of battle. Was he living or dead, — well or wounded? Who could tell him? and what tale could he bear to the mother? These were questions which knocked at the father's heart, drove sleep from his eyelids, and made him, for the first time in his life, a woman. All night long he walked the camp, questioning the stragglers who came in from the front, or the fugitives who had escaped from the clutches of the enemy. But they brought no tidings of Willie. The hospital was taken, they said, and no doubt the boy was captured. This was all that the father learned, though day after day he questioned the new-comers, till his loss was known throughout the army; but he did not give up hope, for something within told him that Willie was living, and would yet be restored to his mother.

At last, after a week had passed, a wounded soldier who had crawled all the way from the Rebel lines came to the camp of the regiment, and said to the Colonel: "I was in the hospital when it was taken. The boy sprung on a horse and tried to get away, but was followed by the rangers, and, the last I saw, was falling to the ground wounded. They must have killed him on the spot, for he gave them a hard ride, and they were a savage set of fellows, — savage as meat-axes."

The next day another came, and he said: "I saw the boy three days ago, lying dead in a Rebel hospital, twelve miles to the southward. He was wounded when taken, and lingered till then, but that day he died, and that night was buried in the timber. I know it was Willie, because he looked just like you, and he said he was the son of a colonel."

The same day another came, and he said: "I know the boy, — a brave little fellow, — and I saw him only two days ago in the Crawfish hospital. When he was captured, his horse fell on him and crushed his right leg to a jelly. They had to take it off above the knee. There are a thousand chances to one against his living through the operation."

Similar accounts were brought by half a score

within the following days, but still the father hoped against hope, for something within him said that his boy was safe, and would yet be restored to his mother.

At last, when a fortnight had gone by with no certain tidings of Willie, Captain Pratt, one of the officers of the regiment, came to the Colonel's tent one morning, and said to him: "I have good news for you. Willie will be back by sunset. You may depend upon it, for in a dream last night I saw him entering your tent, alive and as well as ever.

The Colonel had little faith in dreams, and is very far from being himself a dreamer; but the confident prediction of the Captain, according as it did with his own hopes, made a powerful impression on him. All day long he sat in his tent, listening to the sound of every approaching footstep, and watching the lengthening shadows as the sun journeyed down to the western hills. At last the great light touched the tops of the far-off trees, and the father's heart sunk within him; but then—when his last hope was going out—a quick step and a glad shout sounded outside, and Willie burst into the tent followed by one half of the regiment. The boy threw his arms about his father's neck, and then the bronzed Colonel,

who had so often ridden unmoved through the storm
of shot and shell, bowed his head and wept; for
this his son was dead, and was alive again, — was
lost, and was found.

3 *

THE OHIO BOY.

I AM now going to tell you about a little boy who worked his own way to manhood. He was very poor, — few of you are so poor, — but he rose to be one of the foremost men of Ohio. As he rose so can you rise, if you do as he did ; that is, work, and improve your opportunities of gaining knowledge. It is to show you the power of work and the worth of knowledge, that I tell you his story.

On the 19th of November, 1831, he was born in a little log cottage in the depths of the Ohio wilderness. Ohio then was not the great State it is now : its settlements were few and far between, and a large portion of its surface was covered with great forests. Right in the midst of one of these forests stood the little log cottage, miles away from any other dwelling.

It was a little cottage, — only eighteen feet one way and thirty feet the other, — and was built of rough logs to which the bark and moss still were clinging. Its door was of plank, swinging on stout iron hinges, and it had two small windows, a floor of split saplings, hewn smooth with an axe, and a roof covered with pine slabs, and held down by long cleats fastened to the timbers. The spaces between the logs were filled in with clay, and the chimney was of sticks laid in mud, and went up on the outside something in the shape of the Egyptian pyramids. If not altogether a mud hovel, there was a great deal of mud about it; but it was cool in summer, and warm in winter, and quite as much of a house as was then to be found in that region.

It held, too, all that the little boy had in the world, — his father, his mother, his two sisters, and his brother; and they were a happy family, — happy because united; for the distance which divided them from the rest of the world brought them nearer to one another, bound them together like separate spires in a sheaf of wheat, with different characters, but with only one life.

But an autumn wind blew, and the sheaf was rent asunder. Before the little boy was two years old, the strong, broad-breasted man who bound these lives together was borne out of the low doorway, and laid in a corner of the little wheat-field forever. Nothing now remained to bind up the drooping spires but the weak, puny arms of the mother;

yet she threw them about the broken sheaf, and once more it stood up to meet the storms of winter, — and it was a cold, hard winter, and they were alone in the wilderness. The snow lay deep all over the hills; and often, when lying awake at night in his mother's narrow bed, the little boy would hear the wolves howling hungrily around the little cabin, and the panthers crying and moaning before the door, like children who had lost their way in a forest.

One night, in the midst of a terrible storm, a heavy drift burst open the door, and piled great heaps of snow all over the lower floor of the little dwelling. The mother sprang out of bed, for she saw the danger, — the wolves would be upon them as soon as they detected the opening! She was a fragile little woman, and her arms were weak; but all at once they grew strong, with the lives of her children. Seizing the big back-log, which was smouldering on the hearth, she bore it to the doorway, and, piling dry fagots upon it, lighted a great fire on the snow. The strong wind fanned the flame, and soon it blazed up, scaring the wolves away. All night long she piled the fagots on the fire, and in the morning cleared away the snow and closed the door. After that they slept in safety.

The long, dreary winter wore away at last, but spring brought no fair weather to the little household. They were not only poor, but in debt. The debt must be paid, and the future — ah! that stared darkly in their faces. But the brave mother went to work bravely. Fifty acres of the little farm of eighty acres were sold, and they set at work upon the remainder. Thomas, who was twelve, hired a horse, and ploughed and sowed the little plat of cleared land; and the mother split the rails, and fenced in the little house-lot. The maul was so heavy that she could only just get it to her shoulder, and with every blow she came down to the ground; but she struggled on with the work, and soon the lot was fenced, and the little farm in tolerable order.

But the corn was running low in the bin, and it was a long time to the harvest. Starvation at last looked in, like a gaunt wolf, at the doorway. This wolf could not be frightened away with fire, but the mother went out bravely to meet him. She measured out the corn, counted what her children would eat, and went to bed without her supper. For weeks she did this; but the children were young and growing; their little mouths were larger than she had measured, and after a while she forgot to eat her dinner also. One meal a day! Think of

it, ye children who have such a mother, and build
to her such a monument as these children have
built to theirs, — pure, true, and useful lives.

So this brave woman and her children drew slav-
ish breath, while forty miles of free air was all above
and about them. But neighbors gathered round the
little log cottage in the wilderness. The nearest was
a mile away ; but a mile in a new country is not half
so long as a mile in an old one, and they came
often to visit the poor widow. They had sewing to
do, and she did it ; ploughing to do, and Thomas
did that ; and, after a time, one of them hired the
boy to work on his farm, paying him twelve dollars
a month for fourteen hours' daily labor. Thomas
worked away like a man ; and — while I do not state
it as a fact for history, — I verily believe that no
man ever was so proud and happy as he when he
came home and counted out into his mother's lap
his first fortnight's wages, all in silver half-dollars !

"Now, mother," he said, "the shoemaker can
·come and make James some shoes."

James was the little boy about whom I am writing ; and though the earth had made four revolu-
tions since he first set foot upon it, he had never
yet known the warm embrace of shoe-leather.

A school had been started at a village three miles

away, and Thomas wanted the others to attend it;
so he worked away with a will to earn money enough
to keep the family through the winter. The shoemaker came at last, and made the shoes, boarding
out a part of his pay; and then Mehitable — the older
sister — took James upon her back, and they all
trudged off to school together, — all but Thomas.
He stayed at home to finish the barn, thrash the
wheat, shell the corn, and force a scanty living for
them all from the little farm of thirty acres.

The village, as I have said, was three miles away.
It was then not much of a village, — only a school-
house, a grist-mill, and a little log store and dwelling, — though now it is a thriving place with a thousand people, and rejoicing in the name of Chagrin
Falls. An odd name you may think, but it has a
meaning. The emigrant Yankee who settled the
village built the mill in the winter, when the stream,
which forms the falls, was a foaming torrent; but
summer came, and lo! the stream stopped running,
and the falls stopped falling; and with the little water remaining he baptized it Chagrin Falls. Very
many of us build mills that grind our grist only half
of the year, but not all of us are honest enough to
thus publish our chagrin to the world. But this is
rather a roundabout way of stating the simple fact,

that when the colder weather came, and the snow
lay deep in the roads, Mehitable was not stout
enough to carry her little brother to school, and so
he staid at home and learned to read at' his mother's knee.

He was a mere scrap of a boy, not five years old,
and only able to spell through his words, when one
day he came across a little poem about the rain. After patient effort he made out this line:

"The rain came pattering on the roof."

"Pattering on the roof!" he shouted; "why,
mother! I've heard the rain do that myself!" All
at once it broke upon him that words stand for
thoughts; and all at once a new world opened to
him, — a world in which poor boys are of quite as
much consequence as rich men, and it may be of a
trifle more, for nearly all the work and thinking of
the world has been done by poor boys. Well, this
new world opened to him; and though a mere scrap
of a boy, he set himself zealously to work to open
the door which leads into it. Before he was out of
bed in the morning he had a book in his hand; and
after dark — the family being too poor to burn candles — he would stretch himself upon the naked
hearth, and, by the light of the fire, spell out the
big words in Bartlett's Reader, until he had the

whole book in his memory, and there it remains to this day.

Seeing his fondness for learning, his mother determined to do all she could to gratify it; and thinking him still too young to trudge three miles to school, she called the neighbors together, and offered them a corner of her little farm if they would build upon it a school-house. It would be as far away from the homes of most of them as the other was, but they caught the spirit of the little woman, and in the course of the autumn the great trees bowed their heads, climbed upon one another's backs, and became a school-house. It was only twenty feet square, and had a puncheon floor, a slab roof, and log-benches without backs or a soft spot to sit on; but it was to turn out men and women for the nation.

Before the winter set in the schoolmaster came, — an awkward, slab-sided young man, rough as the bark, and green as the leaves of the pine-trees which grew about his home in New Hampshire; but, like the pines, he had a wonderful deal of sap in him, — a head crammed with knowledge, and a heart full of good feeling. He was to "board around" among the neighbors, and at first was quartered at the little cottage, to eat the widow's corn-bread, and sleep in

E

the loft with James and Thomas. He took at once
a fancy to James, and as the little fellow trotted
along by his side on the first day of school, he put
his hand upon his head, and said to him: "If you
learn, my boy, you may grow up and be a general."

The boy did not know exactly what it was to be
a general; but his mother had told him about the
red and blue coats of the Revolution, and of their
brass buttons and gilded epaulets, so he fancied it
must be some very grand thing; and he answered,
"O yes, sir! I'll learn, — I'll be a general."

It was one of the rules of the school, — and I believe it is of every school, — that the scholars should
sit still and not gaze about the school-room. But
James never sat still in all his life. He had a gal-
vanic battery in his brain which let off an electric
shock every other minute, jerking his arms and legs
about like a dancing Jack's when pulled by a string;
and when put upon the rough log benches he kept
up the movements.

"Sit still, James," said the teacher, noticing his
uneasy motions. "Yes, sir," answered the little
boy, and he tried hard to do it; but "Sit *still*,
James," again, after a while, said the teacher, and
"Yes, sir," again answered the little boy; and again
he tried to do it, and tried so hard that he minded

nothing else, and entirely neglected to study. The result was that his lessons were not learned, and after a few days the teacher said to his mother, "I don't want to wound you, ma'am; but I fear I can make nothing of James. He won't sit still, and he does n't learn his lessons."

But he did wound the little woman; nothing had wounded her so much since the death of her husband. Bursting into a flood of tears, she cried: "O James!" This was all she said, but it went to the heart of the five-year-old boy. He thought he was very wicked, that he had done very wrong, and burying his face in her lap, he sobbed out: "O mother! I'm so sorry! I will be a good boy! I will sit still! I will learn!"

The sorrow of the child touched the heart of the teacher; and he tried him again, and tried him in the right way. He let him move about as much as he liked, calling to mind that he came to school to become a scholar, not a block of wood. At the end of a fortnight he said to the widow: "James is perpetual motion; but he learns, — not a scholar in the school learns so fast as he." This cured the mother's sorrow; for she had set her heart upon this boy becoming a. man of learning.

This restlessness was a characteristic of the boy.

It was born in him, and clings to him even now that he is a man. Every night when lying.in his narrow bed, in the little cottage, he would kick off the clothes, and turning over, half awake, say to his brother, "Thomas, cover me up." A quarter of a century later, with General Sheridan he lay down one night on the ground after a great battle, with only a single blanket between them. His eyes were no sooner closed than, after his usual fashion, he kicked off the clothes, and turning over, half awake, said to Sheridan, "Thomas, cover me up." Sheridan covered him up, and in doing so awakened him, and repeated the words he had said. Then the man, who all that day had ridden unmoved through a hurricane of bullets, turned his face away, and wept like a child, for he thought of Thomas, and of the little log cottage in the wilderness.

When the term was over, the teacher gave James a Testament, — his way of saying that, for his years, he was the best scholar in the school. He took it home, and I verily believe that the little cottage then held the happiest mother on this continent; for the little woman thought she saw in her home-spun boy one of the future men who were to sway this nation.

So things went on, — Thomas tilling the farm or

working for the neighbors, and James going to
school and helping his brother mornings and evenings, until one was twelve and the other twenty-one
years old. Then, wanting to make more money
than he could at home, Thomas went to Michigan,
and engaged in clearing land for a farmer. In a
few months he returned with seventy-five dollars all
in gold. Counting it out on the little pine table,
he said, "Now, mother, you shall have a framed
house."

All these years they had lived in the little log
cottage, but Thomas had been gradually cutting the
timber, getting out the boards, and gathering together the other materials, for a new dwelling; and
now it was to go up, and his mother have a comfortable home for the rest of her days. Soon a
carpenter was hired, and they set to work upon it.
James took so handily to the business that the joiner
said to him, "You were born to be a carpenter."
This gave the boy an idea. "Shall Thomas," he
said to himself, "make so much money for mother,
and I make none? No. I'll set up for a carpenter, and buy her some chairs, a bedstead, and a ma-
hogany bureau,"— and straightway he did it.

During the next two years he built four or five
barns, going to school only at intervals; and then

had learned all that is to be learned from Kirkham's Grammar, Pike's and Adams's Arithmetics, and Morse's (old) Geography, — that wonderful book which describes Albany as a city with a great many houses, and a great many people, "all standing with their gable ends to the street." With this immensity of knowledge he thought he would begin the world. Not having got above a barn, he naturally concluded he was *not* "born to be a carpenter," and so cast about for some occupation better suited to his genius. One — about its suitableness I will not venture an opinion — was not long in presenting itself.

About ten miles from his mother's house, and not far away from Cleveland, lived a man who had founded a village, and done his best to get his name into history. He was unable to write it, but what of that? other people could, and if he gave it to the village they would print it in the newspapers, from whence it would get into the geographies, and finally creep by the back door into history. It was an ugly name; but it was the best the man had, and might sound better at the distance of a century; and the village was a little village, but it might grow, — in fact it was growing, — so without being considered a dreamer, its founder might indulge in dreams of a moderate immortality. The village was growing, for James had just added a wood-shed to the half-dozen log shanties of which it was composed; and so it came about that he met its proprietor, and the current of his life was changed, —diverted into one of those sterile by-ways in which currents will now and then run, without being able to give any good reason for so useless a proceeding.

"You kin read, you kin write, and you are death on figgers," said the man to the boy one day, as he watched the energetic way in which he did his work; "so stay with me, keep my 'counts, 'tend to the saltery, and travil round, gittin' up the ashes and dickerin' off the tin-ware. I'll find you, and give you fourteen dollars a month."

Fourteen dollars a month was an immense sum to a boy of his years, so that night he trudged off through the woods to consult his mother. The little woman was naturally pleased that the services of her son were so highly valued; but she had misgivings about the proposed occupation, — a world of wickedness, she thought, lurked between buying and selling.

"That may be, mother," said the boy, "but because it makes other people rogues, should it make me one? I shall see the world (ten square miles of woods, and ten log-houses), and besides, the house needs painting, and I do so want to build you a piazza."

"I can do without the paint or the piazza," replied the little woman. "I want you to go on with your studies. Some day, if you do, you may be as great a preacher as Hosea Ballou."

Hosea Ballou was a near relative of the family, and that, I presume, proves that preaching runs in the blood, for the boy afterwards took to it as naturally as a duck takes to water.

"But, mother," rejoined the lad, "Thomas is working too hard. My fourteen dollars a month will give him a chance to play a little."

Ah! the tact and logic of unselfish boyhood! This little speech broke down the barricade of prudence behind which the mother had intrenched herself; and after a momentary struggle she surrendered. "Very well, my son," she said, "let it be as you say; only be a good boy and come home as often as you can."

And thus our hero became prime minister to a blacksalter. With a two-horse wagon he ranged the country, bartering away tin-pans, and gathering up wood-ashes. To this useful pursuit he applied the rules of arithmetic and the principles of grammar. And he did it well. So many ashes never were sold, so many tin-kettles never were bought, and so much good grammar never was heard by the simple housewives of that region, as during the two years that he flourished his whip about the black-salter's wagon. He won the hearts and emptied the pockets of every old man and old woman within a circuit of ten miles of the little village at the cross-roads. One of them wrote to me, when I was gathering materials for this little history, " I always loved the lad ; and I remember telling on him once, that if he 'd run for Congress I 'd vote for him, and I done it. He was a Black-Republican, and I a born Democrat ; but I help put him where he is, and I 'll do it again, no matter what he goes for."

The founder of the village, though a little weak on the subject of immortality, had a keen eye to his mortal interests. He thoroughly appreciated the tact, good sense, and restless activity of his homespun assistant, and he would occasionally say to him, in his rough but hearty fashion : "You 're a good boy. Keep on, and one of these days you 'll have a saltery of your own ; and, may be, somewhere out West be called after a village as big as our'n."

And so he might, had not good or bad fortune thrown in his way the few choice works which com-

4

prised the blacksalter's library. These books, selected by the daughter of the village, — who wrote
"poetry" for a Cleveland newspaper, and therefore
had some literary taste, — were such standard produc-
tions as "Sinbad the Sailor," "The Lives of Eminent Criminals," "Two Ways of Marrying a Wife,"
"Rinaldo Rinaldini," "The Pirate's Own Book,"
and Marryatt's Novels. Totally different from the
dry but wholesome reading on which he had been
nurtured, they roused the imagination, and fostered
the love of adventure which was born in the back-
woods boy. But soon an event occurred which
threw him upon the world these books told about,
and taught him that "all is not gold that glitters,"
and life not a gorgeous romance "full of sound and
fury, signifying nothing."

The blacksalter's daughter had attended school at
Cleveland, and, coming home, had drawn within her
narrow orbit one of the Professors of the Seminary,
who afterwards revolved round her as regularly as
the moon revolves round the earth, his feet coming
into conjunction with her father's andirons every Saturday night precisely as the sun sunk below the ho-
rizon. The mother was immensely pleased with
these astronomical movements, for she was a woman
of lofty aspirations, and, above all things, desired to

see her daughter in matrimonial relations with one
of those heavenly bodies that move about the earth
in black "store-coats," white cravats, and shining calf-
skins. She looked for the coming of the Professor
as we look for the return of a comet; and, on such
occasions, dismissing her husband and his assistant
to some remote part of the house, would array herself
in her best Turkey calico, and add her own irresisti-
ble magnetism to the powerful attraction of her
daughter.

That calico was a wonderful calico. Of flaming
red and yellow, covered over with huge horns of
plenty, — all, by the odd taste of the wearer, turned
upside down, and spilling their roses and dollars
upon the ground, — it was enough to terrify a wolf,
or a wild-buffalo. But it did not terrify the Professor. He insisted that in it she looked like Venus
just rising from the sea; but to other eyes she re-
sembled, as it hung about her gaunt, bony figure,
and stood out in strong relief against her jaundiced
complexion, a barber's pole rigged out for a holiday.

Well, regular as the moon, the Professor appeared
every Saturday night at sunset; but the moon now
and then suffers an eclipse, and once, and once
only, the Professor did come after dark. The family

had given him up for the night, and its plebeian members had been admitted to the sitting-room, — which, by the way, was drawing-room, living-room, wash-room, and kitchen, all combined, — and the master of the house had taken his usual seat before the fire, and James, in his work-day clothes, smeared with black-lye and ashes, had sunk into his accustomed nook in the chimney-corner, when the door opened, and the "store-coat" and calf-skins came into conjunction with the andirons. The luminary was more than ordinarily brilliant that night, and soon began to blaze away about the "fathers" in a fashion which would have scorched the beards of those worthies had they been present. All this was "stunning" to the country lad, who, with ears, eyes, and mouth wide open, sat there swallowing every rocket that went off, until the red calico, which had moved about uneasily for some time, at last jerked out, in a sentence bristling with exclamation-points, "Husband! hain't it time that servants was abed!"

"Servants!" He a servant! He, who had read all about the battle of Bunker Hill! whose great-grandfather had seen a signer of the Declaration of Independence! *He* a servant! How the blood boiled in his veins, rushed to his face, and tingled way down to the tips of his toes! O that a man

had said it! But it was a woman; so his hands and
feet were tied. With the latter, however, he managed
to bound up the rickety ladder which did duty as
a stairway; and then, burying his face in the bed-
clothes, he cried the night away.

In the morning he announced to the blacksalter
that a boy and a bundle of clothes were about to be
subtracted from the population of his village. The
worthy man saw the main prop of his fortunes falling,
and demeaned himself accordingly. But entreaties
and remonstrances were alike unavailing. Outraged
dignity could be appeased only by an apology, and
a change of manners on the part of the red calico.
But the colors of Turkey red, and the manners of
shallow old women, are unchangeable; so in half
an hour our hero, with his little bundle slung over
his shoulder, was on his way homeward. His mother
received him with open arms and a blessing. " Providence," she said, "will open some better way for
you, my son." And Providence did; but it took its
own time and way about it.

Now the virus the boy had imbibed from the
blacksalter's books began to work. He determined
to go out into the great world, and to carve out a
destiny — where carving is easy — on the breast of
the waters. His mother opposed this; but finally

said that he might go to Cleveland, view the grand city, and return at once if he could not procure some respectable employment. So, with ten dollars of his little earnings in his pocket, and his small bundle of clothes over his shoulder, he set out in a few days on the journey.

He arrived at Cleveland just at dark, and after a good night's sleep and a warm breakfast went out to view the city. It was scarcely a fourth of its present size; but to the boy it was an immensity of houses. He had never seen buildings half so large, nor steeples half so high; in fact, he had never seen steeples at all, for the simple people among whom he had lived did not put cocked hats and cockades upon their meeting-houses. He wandered about all day, stepping now and then into the business places to inquire for employment; but no one wanted an honest lad who could read, write, and was "death on figgers." Everybody could read and write, and there was no end to their figuring, — so said a good-natured gentleman, who gratuitously advised the boy to go home, teach a district school, or do honest work for a living.

Night found him, weary and footsore, down upon the docks, among the shipping. "These," he said to himself, as he looked around on the fleet of little sloops and schooners, "are the great ships that Captain Marryatt tells about"; and visions of Midshipman Easy, with a wife in every port, and of Japhet searching for a father, and finding only lewd adventures, danced before his eyes, and made him long for a free life upon the water. He sat down on the head of a pier, and looked out on the great lake, heaving and foaming and rolling in broken waves all about him. He watched it creeping up the white beach, and gliding back, singing a low hymn among the shining pebbles, or muttering hoarse cries to the black rocks along the shore; and then looked out on the white sails dancing about all over its bosom. His mother's little cottage, and the little woman herself—even then, it may be, seated in the open doorway, looking up the road for his coming—faded from his sight as he gazed, and—he stepped down upon one of the tossing vessels.

It was a dirty fore-and-aft schooner, with ragged sails, a greasy deck, and a low, sunken cabin. In this cabin, which was thick with tobacco-smoke, about a dozen men, with reeking clothes and sooty faces, were drinking and carousing. A dirt-bedraggled woman sat in one corner; and on a shelf in another, among a score of brandy-bottles, stood the boy's old friends, "Rinaldo Rinaldini," and "Sinbad

the Sailor." This surely was not the life he had
seen in his dreams; but he was not a boy who ever
went backward. Boldly he went down; his foot was
on the last step, and he was about to accost the
sailors, when there, right out of the blue tobacco-
smoke, came a vision that held his foot to the floor,
and his tongue to the roof of his mouth, as if bound
by a palsy. It was a little log cottage and a little
pale-faced woman! The bones were starting from
her flesh, but with her wasted hand she was dealing
out her last morsel of food to her children. The
boy gazed, and for the first time in his life went
backward. O, mighty power of mother's love, which
can thus stretch its arms across leagues of country,
and save the life it has created!

He lingered about the streets on the following
day, unable to tear himself from the strange sights
all about him; and it was long after noon before he
set out on his weary walk homeward. The morning
had been clear and pleasant; but the evening came
on with dark, heavy clouds filling all the heavens.
Toward night he entered a forest, and soon the wind
sighing among the trees, and low mutterings sounding afar off on the lake, told him that a storm was
coming. He pressed rapidly on to find the shelter
of some house, but no house appeared, and after

a while the rain came down in torrents. It wet him through and through, but he kept on, not daring to take refuge under the trees; for he had heard that the lightning, drawn by their slender tops, often came down and left the footsore traveller forever by the wayside.

It was now pitch dark, and the road grew wet and miry, and his legs weak and weary with walking. At last he came to a bridge, over what seemed to be a deep and wide river. Laying down his bundle, he leaned against the railing of the bridge, and took a long look up and down the stream. It was broad, but too straight for a river. Ah! now he remembered! He had come further than he counted. It was the canal, and there, far off in the distance, was a light moving towards him. It was a boat, and it would give him shelter from the storm which then was raging even more furiously than ever. It would take him out of his way, but he could come back in the morning. That would be better than staying all night in the storm; and go on he could not. It was a weary while; but at last the black outlines of the boat crept out of the darkness, and glided under the bridge on which he was standing. A moment more, and he had dropped upon its deck, and entered its little cabin.

The Captain of the boat received him kindly; furnished him a warm supper, a suit of dry clothes, and, in the morning, proposed to take him into his employment, and to pay him "sixteen dollars a month and found,"— man's wages.

The boy consented, and so he rose — it may have been an Irish hoist — from the station of prime minister to a blacksalter to the post of driver of a canal-boat. He held this position five months; and then an event occurred which changed the whole current of his life, gave him a purpose, and made him a man.

One rainy midnight, as the boat was leaving one of the long reaches of slack-water which abound in the Ohio and Pennsylvania Canal, he was called up to take his turn in attending the bowline. Tumbling out from his bunk, his eyes heavy with sleep, he took his stand on the narrow platform below the bow-deck, and began uncoiling the line to be in readiness to work the boat through a lock it was approaching. Slowly and sleepily he unwound the coil until it kinked and caught in a narrow cleft in the edge of the deck. He gave it a sudden pull, but it held fast; then another and a stronger pull, and it gave way, but sent him backward over the bow of the boat into the water. Down he went into

the dark night, and the still darker river, and the
boat glided on to bury him among the fishes. No
human help was near; God only could save him, and
He only by a miracle! So the boy thought as he
went down, saying the prayer his mother had taught
him. Instinctively clutching the rope he sank below the surface, when he felt it tighten in his grasp,
and hold firmly. Seizing it hand over hand, he
drew himself up on deck, and was again a live boy
among the living. Another kink had caught in another crevice, and saved him. Was it that prayer,
or the love of his praying mother, which had wrought
this miracle? He did not know; but long after the
boat passed the lock, he stood there, in his dripping
clothes, pondering the question.

Coiling the rope again, he attempted to throw it
again into the crevice; but it had lost the knack of
kinking. Many times he tried, — six hundred, says
my informant, — and then sat down and reflected.
"I have thrown this rope," he said to himself, "six
hundred times, — I might throw it ten as many times
without its catching. Ten times six hundred are
six thousand; so, there were six thousand chances
against my life. Against such odds, it could have
been saved only by what mother calls Providence.
Providence, therefore, thinks it worth saving; and

if that's so, I'll not throw it away on a canal-boat.
I'll go home, get an education, and become a man."

Straightway he acted on this resolution, and not
long afterward stood before the little cottage in the
wilderness. It was late at night; the stars were out,
and the moon was down; but by the fire-light which
shone through the window he saw his mother kneeling before an open book which lay on a chair in the
corner. She was reading, but her eyes were off the
page, looking up to the Invisible. "O turn unto
me," she said, "and have mercy upon me; give thy
strength unto thy servant, and save the son of thine
handmaid." More she read which sounded like a
prayer; but this is all that the boy remembers. He
opened the door, put his arm about her neck, and
his head upon her bosom. What words he spoke I
do not know; but there, by her side, he gave back
to God the life which he had given. So the mother's prayer was answered; so sprang up the seed
which, in toil and tears, she had planted.

Then the boy set about securing an education.
While Thomas took care of his mother, he worked
his way through college with a saw and a jack-plane,
and at twenty-five was chosen President of the Col-
legiate Institution at Hiram, Ohio. At twenty-seven
he was elected to the Senate of his native State;

but, before his term expired, the war broke out, and
Governor Dennison offered him the command of a
regiment. He went home, opened his mother's Bible,
and pondered upon the subject. He had then a
wife, a child, and a few thousand dollars. If he gave
his life to the country, would God and the few thousand dollars provide for his wife and child? He
consulted the Book about it. It seemed to answer
in the affirmative ; and, before morning, he wrote to
a friend : " I regard my life as given to the country.
I am only anxious to make as much of it as possible, before the mortgage on it is foreclosed."

Thus, with a life not his own, he went into the
war, and on the sixteenth of December, 1861, he
was given command of the little army which held
Kentucky to her moorings in the Union.

He knew nothing of war beyond its fundamental
principles ; which are, you know, that a big boy can
whip a little boy ; and that one big boy can whip
two little boys, if he take them singly, one after the
other. He knew no more about it ; and yet he was
called upon to solve a military problem which has
puzzled the heads of the greatest generals ; namely,
how two small bodies of men, stationed widely apart,
can unite in the presence of an enemy, and beat him,
when he is of twice their united strength, and strongly

posted behind intrenchments? With the help of many "good men and true," he solved this problem; and, in telling how he solved it, I shall relate one of the most remarkable exploits of the war of the Rebellion.

Humphrey Marshall, with five thousand men, had invaded Kentucky. Entering it at Pound Gap, he had fortified a strong natural position near Paintville, and, with small bands, was overrunning the whole Piedmont region. This region, containing an area larger than the whole of Massachusetts, was occupied by about four thousand blacks and a hundred thousand whites, — a brave, hardy, rural population, with few schools, scarcely any churches, and only one newspaper; but with that sort of patriotism which grows among mountains, and clings to its barren hillsides, as if they were the greenest spots in the universe. Among this simple people Marshall was scattering firebrands. Stump orators were blazing away at every cross-road, lighting a fire which threatened to sweep Kentucky from the Union. That done, — so early in the war, — dissolution might have followed.

To the Ohio canal boy was committed the task of extinguishing this conflagration. It was a difficult task, one which, with the means at command, would have appalled any man not made equal to it by early struggles with hardship and poverty, and entire trust in the Providence that guards his country.

The means at command were twenty-five hundred men, divided into two bodies, and separated by sixty miles of mountain country. This country was infested with guerrillas, and occupied by a disloyal people. The sending of despatches across it was next to impossible; but communication being opened, and the two columns set in motion, there was danger they would be fallen on, and beaten in detail, before they could form a junction. This was the great danger. What remained — the beating of five thousand Rebels, posted behind intrenchments, by half their number of Yankees, operating in the open field — seemed to the young Colonel less difficult of accomplishment.

Evidently, the first thing to be done was to find a trustworthy messenger to convey despatches between the two halves of the Union army. To this end, the Ohio boy applied to the Colonel of the 14th Kentucky.

"Have you a man," he asked, "who will die, rather than fail or betray us?"

The Kentuckian reflected a moment, then answered: "I think I have, — John Jordan, from the head of Blaine." *

Jordan was sent for. He was a tall, gaunt, sallow man of about thirty; with small gray eyes, a fine, falsetto voice, pitched in the minor key, and his speech the rude dialect of the mountains. His face had as many expressions as could be found in a regiment, and he seemed a strange combination of cunning, simplicity, undaunted courage, and undoubting faith; yet, though he might pass for a simpleton, he talked a quaint sort of wisdom which ought to have given his name to history.

The young Colonel sounded him thoroughly; for the fate of the little army might depend on his fidelity. The man's soul was as clear as crystal, and in ten minutes James saw right through him. His history is stereotyped in that region. Born among the hills, where the crops are stones, and sheep's noses are sharpened before they can nibble the thin grass between them, his life had been one of the hardest toil and privation. He knew nothing but what Nature, the Bible, the "Course of Time," and two or three of Shakespeare's plays had taught him; but somehow in the mountain air he had grown to

* The Blaine is a small stream which puts into the Big Sandy, a short distance from the town of Louisa, Ky.

be a man, — a man a   d   the angels account
manhood.

"Why did you co   he war?" at last asked
James.

"To do my sheer fur the kentry, Gin'ral," answered the man; "and I did n't druv no barg'in
wi' th' Lord. I guv him my life squar out; and ef
he 's a mind ter tuck it on this tramp, — why, it 's
a his'n; I 've nothin' ter say ag'in it."

"You mean that you 've come into the war not
expecting to get out of it!"

"That 's so, Gin'ral."

"Will you die rather than let the despatch be
taken?"

"I will."

James recalled what had passed in his own mind
when poring over his mother's Bible that night at
his home in Ohio; and it decided him. "Very
well," he said; "I will trust you."

The despatch was written on tissue paper, rolled
into the form of a bullet, coated with warm lead,
and put into the hand of the Kentuckian. He was
given a carbine, a brace of revolvers, and the fleetest horse in his regiment, and, when the moon was
down, started on his perilous journey. He was to
ride at night, and hide in the woods or in the houses

of loyal men in the ████ ███ It was pitch dark when
he set out; but he knew ███ inch of the way, having travelled it often, ██ ███ mules to market. He
had gone twenty miles by ██ly dawn, and the house
of a friend was only a few miles beyond him. The
man himself was away; but his wife was at home,
and she would harbor him till nightfall. He pushed
on, and tethered his horse in the timber; but it was
broad day when he rapped at the door, and was admitted. The good woman gave him breakfast, and
showed him to the guest's chamber, where, lying
down in his boots, he was soon in a deep slumber.

The house was a log cabin in the midst of a few
acres of deadening, — ground from which trees have
been cleared by girdling. Dense woods were all
about it; but the nearest forest was a quarter of a
mile distant, and, should the scout be tracked, it
would be hard to get away over this open space,
unless he had warning of the approach of his pursuers. The woman thought of this, and sent up
the road, on a mule, her whole worldly possessions,
— an old negro, dark as the night, but faithful as
the sun in the heavens. It was high noon when
the mule came back, his heels striking fire, and his
rider's eyes flashing, as if ignited from the sparks the
steel had emitted.

"Dey'm comin', Missus," he cried, — not half a mile away, — twenty Secesh, — ridin' as ef de Debbel wus arter 'em."

She barred the door, and hastened to the guest's chamber.

"Go," she cried, "through the winder, — ter the woods. They'll be yere in a minnit."

"How many is thar?" asked the scout.

"Twenty, — go, — go at once, — or you'll be taken!"

The scout did not move; but, fixing his eyes on the woman's face, said, —

"Yes, I yere 'em. Thar's a sorry chance for my life a'ready. But, Rachel, I've thet 'bout me thet's wuth more'n my life, — thet, may-be, 'll save Kaintuck. If I'm killed, will ye tuck it ter Colonel Cranor, at McCormick's Gap?'

"Yes, yes, I will! But go; you've not a minnit to lose, I tell you."

"I know, but wull ye swar it, — swar ter tuck this ter Cunnel Cranor, 'fore th' Lord that yeres us?"

."Yes, yes, I will," she said, taking the bullet. But horses' hoofs were already sounding in the dooryard. "It's too late," cried the woman. "O why did you stop to parley?"

"Never mind, Rachel," answered the scout. "Don't

tuck on. Tuck ye keer o' th' despatch. Valu' it loike yer life, — loike Kaintuck. The Lord 's callin' fur me, and I 'm a ready."

But the scout was mistaken. It was not the Lord ; but a dozen devils at the door-way.

"What does ye want?" asked the woman, going to the door.

"The man as come from Garfield's camp at sun-up, — John Jordan, from the head o' Blaine," answered a voice from the outside.

"Ye karn't hev him fur th' axin'," said the scout. "Go away, or I 'll send some o' ye whar the weather is warm, I reckon."

"Pshaw!" said another voice, — from his speech one of the chivalry. "There are twenty of us. We 'll spare your life, if you give up the despatch ; if you don't, we 'll hang you higher than Haman."

This was in the beginning of the war, when swarms of spies infested every Union camp, and treason was only a gentlemanly pastime, not the serious business it has grown to be since traitors are no longer dangerous.

"I 've nothing but my life thet I 'll guv up," answered the scout ; "and ef ye tuck thet, ye 'll hev ter pay the price, — six o' yourn."

"Fire the house!" shouted one.

"No, don't do thet," said another. "I know him, — he's cl'ar grit, — he'll die in the ashes; and we won't git the despatch."

This sort of talk went on for half an hour; then there was a dead silence, and the woman went to the loft, from which she could see all that was passing on the outside. About a dozen of the horsemen were posted around the house; but the remainder, dismounted, had gone to the edge of the woods, and were felling a well-grown sapling, with the evident intention of using it as a battering-ram to break down the front door.

The woman, in a low tone, explained the situation; and the scout said, —

"It 'r my only chance. I must run fur it. Bring me yer red shawl, Rachel."

She had none, but she had a petticoat of flaming red and yellow. Handling it as if he knew how such articles can be made to spread, the scout softly unbarred the door, and, grasping the hand of the woman, said, —

"Good by, Rachel. It 'r a right sorry chance; but I may git through If I do, I'll come ter-night; if I don't, get ye the despatch ter the Cunnel. Good by."

To the right of the house, midway between it and

the woods, stood the barn. That way lay the route of the scout. If he could elude the two mounted men at the door-way, he might escape the other horsemen; for they would have to spring the barn-yard fences, and their horses might refuse the leap. But it was foot of man against leg of horse, and a "right sorry chance."

Suddenly he opened the door, and dashed at the two horses with the petticoat. They reared, wheeled, and bounded away like lightning just let out of harness. In the time that it takes to tell it, the scout was over the first fence, and scaling the second; but a horse was making the leap with him. His pistol went off, and the rider's earthly journey was over. Another followed, and his horse fell mortally wounded. The rest made the circuit of the barn-yard, and were rods behind when the scout reached the edge of the forest. Once among those thick laurels nor horse nor rider can reach a man if he lies low, and says his prayers in a whisper.

The Rebels bore the body of their comrade back to the house, and said to the woman, "We 'll be revenged for this. We know the route he 'll take; and will have his life before to-morrow; and you — we 'd burn your house over your head, if you were not the wife of Jack Brown."

Brown was a loyal man, who was serving his country in the ranks of Marshall. Thereby hangs a tale, which one day I may tell you. Soon the men rode away, taking the poor woman's only wagon as a hearse for their dead comrade.

Night came, and the owls cried in the woods in a way they had not cried for a fortnight. "T'whoot, t'whoot," they went, as if they thought there was music in hooting. The woman listened, put on a dark mantle, and followed the sound of their voices. Entering the woods, she crept in among the bushes, and talked with the owls as if they had been human.

"They know the road ye'll take," she said, "ye must change yer route. Yere ar' the bullet."

"God bless ye. Rachel," responded the owl, "yer a true 'ooman," and he hooted louder than before, to deceive pursuers, and keep up the music.

"Ar' yer nag safe?" she asked.

"Yes, and good for forty mile afore sun-up."

"Well, yere ar' suthin ter eat; ye'll need it. Good by, and God go wi' ye."

"He'll go wi' ye, fur he loves noble wimmin."

Their hands clasped, and then they parted, — he, to his long ride; she, to the quiet sleep of those who, out of a true heart, serve their country.

The night was dark and drizzly; but before morning the clouds cleared away, leaving a thick mist hanging low on the meadows. The scout's mare was fleet, but the road was rough, and a slosh of snow impeded the travel. He had come by a strange way, and did not know how far he had travelled by sunrise; but lights were ahead, shivering in the haze of the cold, gray morning. Were they the early candles of some sleepy village, or the camp-fires of a band of guerillas? He did not know, and it would not be safe to go on till he did know. The road was lined with trees, but they could give no shelter; for they were far apart, and the snow lay white between them. He was in the blue grass region. Tethering his horse in the timber, he climed a tall oak by the roadside; but the mist was too thick to discern anything distinctly. It seemed, however, to be breaking away, and he would wait until his way was clear; so he sat there, an hour, two hours, and ate his breakfast from the satchel John's wife had slung over his shoulder. At last the fog lifted a little, and he saw, close at hand, a little hamlet, — a few rude huts gathered round a cross-road. No danger could lurk in such a place, and he was about to descend and pursue his journey, when suddenly he heard, up the road by which he came, the rapid tramp of a body of horsemen. The mist was thicker

below, so halfway down the tree he went, and waited
their coming. They moved at an irregular pace,
carrying lanterns, and pausing every now and then
to inspect the road, as if they had missed their way,
or lost something. Soon they came near, and were
dimly outlined in the gray mist, so the scout could
make out their number. There were thirty, — the
original band, and a reinforcement. Again they
halted when abreast of the tree, and searched the
road narrowly.

"He must have come this way," said one, — he
of the chivalry. "The other road is six miles longer, and he would take the shortest route. It 's
an awful pity we did n't head him off on both
roads."

"We kin come up with him yet, ef we turn plumb
round, and foller on t' other road, — whar we lost
the trail, — back thar, three miles ter the deadnin',"
said one of the men.

Now another spoke, and his voice the scout remembered. He belonged to his own company in
the 14th Kentucky. "It 'r so," he said, "he has
tuck that road. I tell ye, I 'd know that mar's
shoe 'mong a million. Nary one loike it wus uver
seed in all Kaintuck, — only a Yankee could ha' invented it."

" And yere it ar'," shouted a man with one of the lanterns, " plain as sun-up."

The 14th Kentuckian clutched the light, and while a dozen dismounted and gathered round, closely examined the shoe track. The ground was bare on the spot, and the print of the horse's hoof was cleanly cut in the half-frozen mud. Narrowly the man looked, and life and death hung on his eyesight. The scout took out the bullet, and placed it in a crotch of the tree. If they took him, the devil should not take the despatch. Then he drew a revolver. The mist was breaking away, and he would surely be discovered, if the men lingered much longer, but he would have the value of his life to the uttermost farthing.

Meanwhile, the horsemen crowded round the footprint, and one of them inadvertently trod upon it. The Kentuckian looked long and earnestly, but, at last, said, " Taint the track. That ar' mar' has a sand-crack on her right fore foot. She did n't take kindly to a round shoe, so the Yank he guv her one with the cork right in the middle o' the quarter. 'T was a durned smart contrivance, fur yer see, it eased the strain, and let the nag go nimble as a squirrel. The cork haint yere, — taint her track, — and we 'se wastin' time in luckin'."

The cork was not there, because the trooper's

tread had obliterated it. Let us thank him for that one good step, if he never take another, for it saved the scout, and, perhaps, it saved Kentucky. When the scout returned that way, he halted abreast of that tree, and examined the ground about it. Right there, in the road, was the mare's track, with the print of the man's foot still upon the inner quarter! He uncovered his head, and from his heart went up a simple thanksgiving.

The horsemen gone, the scout came down from the tree, and pushed on into the misty morning. There might be danger ahead, but there surely was danger behind him. His pursuers were only half convinced they had struck his trail, and some sensible fiend might put it into their heads to divide and follow, part by one route, part by the other.

He pushed on over the sloshy road, his mare every step going slower and slower. The poor beast was jaded out; for she had travelled forty miles, eaten nothing, and been stabled in the timber. She would have given out long before, had her blood not been the best in Kentucky. As it was, she staggered along as if she had taken a barrel of whiskey. Five miles farther on was the house of a Union man. She must reach it or die by the wayside; for the merciful man regardeth not the life of his beast when he carries despatches.

The loyalist did not know the scout, but his honest face secured him a cordial welcome. He explained that he was from the Union camp on the Big Sandy, and offered any price for a horse to go on with.

"Yer nag is wuth ary two o' my critters," said the man. "Ye kin take the best beast I 've got, and when yer ag'in this way, we 'll swop back even."

The scout thanked him, mounted the horse, and rode off into the mist again, without the warm breakfast which the good woman had, half-cooked, in the kitchen. It was eleven o'clock; and at twelve that night he entered Colonel Cranor's quarters at Mc-Cormick's Gap, having ridden sixty miles, with a rope round his neck, for thirteen dollars a month, hard tack, and a shoddy uniform.

The Colonel opened the despatch. It was dated, Louisa, Kentucky, December 24th, midnight; and directed him to move at once with his regiment, (the Fortieth Ohio, eight hundred strong,) to Prestonburgh. He would encumber his men with as few rations and as little luggage as possible, bearing in mind that the safety of his command depended on his expedition. He would also convey the despatch to Lieutenant-Colonel Woolford, at Stamford, and direct him to join the march with his three hundred cavalry.

Hours now were worth months of common time; and, on the following morning, Cranor's column was set in motion. The scout lay by till night, then set out; and, at daybreak, exchanged his now jaded horse for the fresh Kentucky mare, even. He ate the housewife's breakfast, too, and took his ease with the good man till dark; then he set out again, and rode through the night in safety. After that his route was beset with perils. The Providence which so wonderfully guarded his way out seemed to leave him to find his own way in; or, as he expressed it, "Ye see, the Lord, he keered more fur the despatch nor he keered fur me; and 't was nat'ral he should; 'case my life only counted one, while the despatch it stood for all Kaintuck."

Be that as it may, he found his road a hard one to travel. The same gang which followed him out waylaid him back, and one starry midnight he fell among them. They lined the road forty deep, and seeing he could not run the gauntlet, he wheeled his mare and fled backwards. The noble beast did her part; but a bullet struck her, and she fell in the road dying. Then — it was Hobson's choice — he took to his legs, and, leaping a fence, was at last out of danger. Two days he lay in the woods, not daring to come out; but hunger finally forced him

to ask food at a negro shanty. The dusky patriot
loaded him with bacon, brown-bread, and blessings;
and, at night, piloted him to a Rebel barn, where
he enforced the Confiscation act, — to him then "the
higher law," — necessity.

With his fresh horse he set out again; and after
various adventures and hair-breadth escapes, too nu-
merous to mention, and too incredible to believe, —
had not similar things occurred all through the war,
— he entered, one rainy midnight, (the 6th of January,) the little log hut, seven miles from Paintville,
where his commander was sleeping.

He rubbed his eyes, and raised himself upon his
elbow, —

"Back safe?" he asked. "Have you seen Cranor?"

"Yes, Giniral. He can't be more 'n two days ahind
o' me, no how."

"God bless you, Jordan. You have done us a
great service," said James, warmly.

"I thanks ye, Giniral," said the scout, his voice
trembling. "That 's more pay 'n I expected."

Having now followed the scout safely back to
camp, we must go on with the little army. They
are only fourteen hundred men, worn out with marching, but boldly they move down upon Marshall.

False scouts have made him believe they are as strong as he, — and they are ; for every one is a hero, and they are led by a general. The Rebel has five thousand men, — forty-four hundred infantry and six hundred cavalry, besides twelve pieces of artillery, — so he says in a letter to his wife, which General Buell has intercepted and the Ohio boy has in his pocket. Three roads lead to Marshall's position. One at the east bearing down to the river, and along its western bank ; another, a circuitous one, to the west, coming in on Paint Creek, at the mouth of Jenny's Creek, on the right of the village ; and a third between the others, — a more direct route, but climbing a succession of almost impassable ridges. These three roads are held by strong Rebel pickets, and a regiment is outlying at the village of Paintville.

To deceive Marshall as to his real strength and designs, the Ohio boy orders a small force of infantry and cavalry to advance along the river, drive in the Rebel pickets, and move rapidly after them as if to attack Paintville. Two hours after this force goes off, a similar one, with the same orders, sets out on the road to the westward ; and, two hours later still, another small body takes the middle road. The effect is, that the pickets on the first route, being

vigorously attacked and driven, retreat in confusion
to Paintville, and despatch word to Marshall that
the Union army is advancing along the river. He
hurries off a thousand infantry and a battery to re-
sist the advance of this imaginary column. When
this detachment has been gone an hour and a half,
he hears, from the routed pickets on the right, that
the Federals are advancing along the western road.
Countermanding his first order, he now directs the
thousand men and the battery to check the new danger; and hurries off the troops at Paintville to the
mouth of Jenny's Creek, to make a stand there. Two
hours later the pickets on the central route are driven
in, and finding Paintville abandoned, flee precipitately
to the fortified camp, with the story that the Union
army is close at their heels, and occupying Paintville.
Conceiving that he has thus lost the town, Marshall
hastily withdraws the detachment of a thousand men
to his fortified camp; and the Ohio boy, moving
rapidly over the ridges of the central route, occupies
the abandoned position.

So affairs stand on the evening of the 8th of January, when a spy enters the camp of Marshall, with
tidings that Cranor, with thirty-three hundred (!) men,
is within twelve hours' march at the westward. On
receipt of these tidings, the "big boy," — he weighs

three hundred pounds by the Louisville hay-scales,
— conceiving himself outnumbered, breaks up his
camp, and retreats precipitately, abandoning or burning a large portion of his supplies. Seeing the fires,
the Ohio boy mounts his horse, and with a thousand
men enters the deserted camp at nine in the evening,
while the blazing stores are yet unconsumed. He
sends a detachment off to harass the retreat, and
waits the arrival of Cranor, with whom he means to
follow and bring Marshall to battle in the morning.

In the morning Cranor comes, but his men are
footsore, without rations, and completely exhausted.
They cannot move one leg after the other. But the
canal boy is bound to have a fight; and every man
who has strength to march is ordered to come forward. Eleven hundred — among them four hundred
of Cranor's tired heroes — step from the ranks, and
with them, at noon of the 9th, the Ohio boy sets
out for Prestonburg, sending all his available cavalry to follow the line of the enemy's retreat, and
harass and delay him.

Marching eighteen miles, he reaches at nine o'clock
that night the mouth of Abbott's Creek, three miles
below Prestonburg, — he and the eleven hundred.
There he hears that Marshall is encamped on the
same stream, three miles higher up; and throwing

5 *

his men into bivouac, in the midst of a sleety rain, he sends an order back to Lieutenant-Colonel Sheldon, who is left in command at Paintville, to bring up every available man, with all possible despatch, for he shall force the enemy to battle in the morning. He spends the night in learning the character of the surrounding country and the disposition of Marshall's forces; and now again John Jordan comes into action.

A dozen Rebels are grinding at a mill, and a dozen honest men come upon them, steal their corn, and make them prisoners. The miller is a tall, gaunt man, and his clothes fit the scout, as if they were made for him. He is a Disunionist, too, and his very raiment should bear witness against this feeding of his enemies. It does. It goes back to the Rebel camp, and — the scout goes in it. That chameleon face of his is smeared with meal, and looks the miller so well that the miller's own wife might not detect the difference. The night is dark and rainy, and that lessens the danger; but still, he is picking his teeth in the very jaws of the lion, — if he can be called a lion who does nothing but roar like unto Marshall.

Space will not permit me to detail this midnight ramble; but it gave the Ohio boy the exact position of the enemy. They had made a stand, and laid an ambuscade for him. Strongly posted on a semicircular hill, at the forks of Middle Creek, on both sides of the road, with cannon commanding its whole length, and hidden by the trees, they were waiting his coming.

The Union commander broke up his bivouac at four in the morning and began to move forward. Reaching the valley of Middle Creek, he encountered some of the enemy's mounted men, and captured a quantity of stores they were trying to withdraw from Prestonburg. Skirmishing went on until about noon, when the Rebel pickets were driven back upon their main body, and then began the battle. It is not my purpose to describe it; for James has already ably done that, in thirty lines, in his despatch to the Government.

It was a wonderful battle. In the history of this war there is not another like it. Measured by the forces engaged, the valor displayed, and the results which followed, it throws into the shade even the achievements of the mighty hosts which saved the nation. Eleven hundred men, without cannon, charge up a rocky hill, over stumps, over stones, over fallen trees, over high intrenchments, right into the face of five thousand, and twelve pieces of artillery!

For five hours the contest rages. Now the Union forces are driven back; then, charging up the hill, they regain the lost ground, and from behind rocks and trees pour in their murderous volleys. Then again they are driven back, and again they charge up the hill, strewing the ground with corpses. So the bloody work goes on; so the battle wavers till the setting sun, wheeling below the trees, glances along the dense lines of Rébel steel moving down to envelop the weary eleven hundred. It is an awful moment, big with the fate of Kentucky. At its very crisis two figures stand out against the fading sky boldly defined in the foreground.

One is in Union blue. With a little band of heroes about him, he is posted on a projecting rock, which is scarred with bullets, and in full view of both armies. His head is uncovered, his hair streaming in the wind, his face upturned in the darkening daylight, and from his soul is going up a prayer, — a prayer for Sheldon and reinforcements! He turns his eyes to the northward, and his lip tightens, as he throws off his coat, and says to his hundred men, — "Boys, *we* must go at them."

The other is in Rebel gray. Moving out to the brow of the opposite hill, and placing a glass to his eye, he, too, takes a long look to the northward.

He starts, for he sees something which the other, on lower ground, does not distinguish. Soon he wheels his horse, and the word "RETREAT" echoes along the valley between them. It is his last word, for six rifles crack, and the Rebel Major lies on the ground, quivering.

The one in blue looks to the north again, and now, floating proudly among the trees, he sees the starry banner. It is Sheldon and his forces! The long ride of the scout is, at last, doing its work for the nation. On they come like the rushing wind, filling the air with their shouting. The rescued eleven hundred take up the strain, and then, above the swift pursuit, above the lessening conflict, above the last boom of the wheeling cannon, goes up the wild huzza of Victory. The Ohio boy has won the day, and rolled back the disastrous tide which has been sweeping on ever since Big Bethel. In ten days Thomas routs Zollicoffer, and then we have and hold Kentucky.

For this very important service to his country, President Lincoln conferred on James the appointment of Brigadier-General. In the course of sixty days he was ordered to join General Buell, and with him marched to the rescue of Grant at the bloody field of Shiloh. Afterwards he was in many marches and many battles, and, when General Rosecrans assumed command of the army of the Cumberland, was selected to be his chief-of-staff, — a very responsible position, and one seldom given to officers who have not received a regular military education. While acting in that capacity he took part in the disastrous battle of Chickamauga; and, with Generals Gordon Granger and George H. Thomas, saved our army from total route on that bloody field. For his services on that occasion he was highly complimented by General Rosecrans, and promoted to a Major-Generalship by the Government. But he soon resigned, to succeed the Hon. Joshua R. Giddings as representative for his native district in Ohio; and he is now serving his country, and the cause of freedom, on the floor of Congress.

To all these honors and all this usefulness the poor Ohio boy attained, because he worked and improved every opportunity of gaining knowledge. His name is JAMES A. GARFIELD; and whenever you see it, I wish you would remember what I have told you about him, and call to mind that, if you work and study as he has done, you may be as useful as he has been, and rise as high as he has risen.

THE VIRGINIA BOY.

PART I.

SLAVERY.

ONE pleasant day in July, 1864, I took passage
on a steamer running between Washington and
City Point, for a short visit into Virginia. The boat
was crowded with passengers,—furloughed officers re-
joining their regiments, convalescent soldiers returning to their commands, and white and black recruits
going to the front to fill the places of the noble
fellows who had fallen in our long and bloody
struggle with the desperate slave power. Among
the latter were about a hundred and fifty men, re-
cently enlisted in the Thirty-first Regiment of United
States Colored Infantry. They were huddled together on the open bow of the boat; and though
stout, healthy-looking fellows, were a motley group
of all ages, colors, and nationalities.

Among them were free negroes from the North,
freedmen from the South, Indians from the Mohawk
Valley, Malays from farther India, and even a shaved

Chinaman, all the way from the Celestial Empire. Men of every race except the white race, and from every clime except the Arctic regions, were gathered there in a space not more than forty feet square! Here, thought I, is a chance to see the world; to "put a girdle round about the earth in forty minutes," at Uncle Sam's expense, and in a government steamer! It was an opportunity not to be lost; so, leaving my travelling companion to nod himself to sleep in the shade of the pilot-house, I went down among them.

And here let me say to the young reader, who would study human nature and the ways of men, that he must take no stately airs and false dignity out with him into the world. He must leave such things at home, along with his stiff dickey and dandy clothes, or the poorest man he meets will draw himself within his shell, and though the ear be put down ever so close, it will fail to catch the music of his life, — music, it may be, as strange as that which throbs in the tiny lungs of the little sea wanderers which are thrown up along the shore.

Well, I left my dignity behind me, and went down among the black recruits. The first one I accosted was an old man with a seamed face, gray hair, and eyes like two stars blazing through the black folds of a thunder-cloud. "You," I said to him, "are an old man to be in the war."

"I can handle a musket as well as a younger man, sir," he answered. "In a time like this every man of my color, young or old, should be at the front."

This was in our darkest days, before the fall of Atlanta; when Grant sat hand-tied before Petersburg, and Early's greyhounds were chasing Hunter through the Shenandoah Valley, and barking away at the very gates of Washington.

"I am glad to hear you say so," I said, warmly; "such pluck as yours would have freed your race a century ago."

"They've pluck enough," he said. "That is n't what's the matter. It's ignorance. They don't know their own strength. These Southern blacks think because a white man can read and fire a gun that he 's a superior being. I 've been telling them it ain't so; and, now that they have muskets in their hands, they begin to believe me."

"I am told that in their first battle they fight better than white men, because they think the musket makes them invincible."

"Yes, it 's so. I 've seen them go where a white man would n't venture, — these degraded black slaves," — and there was a slight sneer in his tone

H

as he said this, — "that you and I are accustomed
to despise."

"Not *I*, old man," I answered.   "I 've known the
Southern negro almost all my life, and think him of
better blood than the chivalry.   But are not you a
freedman ? "

"No, sir ! " he replied, "I 'm a *free*man ; born free,
in York State, right under the droppings of the sanc-
tuary, — close to Scripture Dick's (Hon. Daniel S.
Dickinson) in Binghampton."

"And you left a comfortable home, at your time of
life, to come out and fight for the rest of your race ? "

"I did.   I stood it till I could n't stand it no
longer, and then I come.   You see, I 'd worked sixty-
one years for myself, and the little rest of my days
I thought I 'd work for my race and my country."

"You are a brave, true man," I answered.   "I
am glad to know you."

"Thank you," he rejoined.   "I am glad to know
you, sir, if you can look below the skin, and detect
the man, whatever his clothes or color."

Continuing the conversation, I learned that the
name of this man was William Pierce ; that he had
been in Washington recruiting for his regiment, and
was then going to City Point with the squad of colored soldiers, — two thirds of whom, he said, were

escaped slaves from Virginia and the Carolinas. On
my remarking, that I wanted to know such of them
as were worth knowing, he said : —

"Ah, yes; you want to crack their cocoa-nuts, —
to get the juice out of them. I always do that myself.
I never meet a man, no matter how poor he is, but
I get some good out of him. That 's the way to
get real learning ; the way to study natur', — human
natur'."

Within the next hour he called a score or more of
his comrades up to the water-tank, on which we were
seated, and I "cracked their cocoa-nuts." Some of
them were tolerably soft, others intolerably hard ; but
all had something in them, which flowed out when
tapped by a free word or a kind look, rich, racy, and
original, as are the utterances of all uncultivated men,
of whatever color.

One, whose story interested me greatly, was a stout,
jovial young fellow, who gave his name as Sam Nich-
ols, and said he had been the slave of a Major Jarvis,
of Louisville, Kentucky. Another was an aged man —
turned of sixty-six — named Henry Washington, who
had belonged to James Blain of Nottaway County,
Virginia. Though so old, he was wearing his country's uniform, and bearing the hardships of the field
in the service of Captain Pitkin, Quartermaster-Gen-

eral of the department. One of his sons, he said, was in the army ; the other — a man "done grown" — had been sold a few years before at Petersburg, and was then languishing his life away at the far South.

The stories of these two men might interest you ; but they would not so well illustrate the life of the Virginia slave, both before and during the war, as the history of a quadroon boy, whom the old Sergeant brought up to me on that greasy hatchway, and who, till far into the night, sat on a low stool in my state-room, living over again his short but strange and eventful career.

He was a youth of about nineteen, with an erect, well-knit frame, glossy black hair, a clear olive complexion, straight, comely features, and an eye like a coal burning at midnight. He was born in a little hut on a plantation not far away from Charlestown, Virginia. The hut was of logs laid up in clay, and it had a mud chimney, an earthen floor, board windows, and a slat door, through which the wind and the overseer could look in of winter nights, and see that the occupants were all snug and warm as they should be.

Besides the boy, the cabin contained an iron crane, a cracked kettle, a half-dozen bricks doing duty as

andirons, a rough bench, a three-legged chair, a few
wooden bowls and spoons, a low bedstead on its
very last legs, another boy blacker than he, but said
to be his brother, and a pale-faced, fragile little woman, who was his mother. This was when the youth
was born. Two weeks later the little woman was
driven to the field to work, and — she never came
back again.

Then the olive-faced boy changed his residence.
He was taken to the children's quarters, — a long,
low, log shanty, where the plantation orphans were
huddled. There he was consigned to the tender
mercies of a toothless hag, whose soul, from long
looking on her own black visage, had caught its
murky hue, — the very blackness of midnight. How
much he suffered from this old woman, how many
blows she made his little back to bear, how many
cold days she drove him shivering away from the
fire, how many winter nights she sent him supperless
to his hard bed on the cabin floor, — the boy did
not know; but he well remembered that one night,
when he was about five years old, she fell over upon
the hearth and was roasted like a partridge. The
older children tried to rescue her; but he went off
into a corner by himself, and falling on his knees,
thanked God that he was about to take the old

hag to heaven, as he took Elijah, in a chariot of flame.

Another old woman took the place of the one who was "translated," and she was some improvement on the last; but her spirit, too, had been soured by long oppression, and the selling away, one by one, of all her children. At times, when the bitter memories came over her, she would vent her bad feelings on the helpless little ones about her; but she attended to their physical wants, and gave them enough to eat, and a warm seat by the winter's fire. And so the little boy grew up, a neglected weed in this great garden of a world.

One day, when he was eight years old, his master came to the cabin with two bewhiskered and bejewelled "gentlemen," and ranging all the children in a row across the floor, he said, "There they are! Take your pick. Five hundred dollars apiece!"

They "picked" half a dozen boys of about his own age, and among them his black "brother," but left him behind. One of the men was disposed to take him, but the other objected that he was "too smart," and so he escaped a journey to the far South and a toilsome life on a sugar plantation, — for these men were negro-traders.

Though so young, he had before this learned that

his master's business was the raising of slaves for market; that he fed and fattened the younger ones, and every year sold off as many as were above five years old; and so made his living by coining into money the blood and bones of beings whose bodies were as strong, and whose souls were as much in the likeness of the Maker, as his own was.

Some few days after the traders went away, the overseer came to the cabin, and asking the old woman for "Yaller Joe," took the boy by the collar, and marched him off to the tobacco-field. There he was set at work from sunrise to sunset; and he went no more to the children's quarter, being sent to lodge with some of the field hands.

This was the first great sorrow of the boy's life; not that he disliked work, but his young heart had wound itself about his little companions; and though he had felt cold and hunger and every grief in the old cabin, it was his home.

But his sorrow, like all the sorrows of childhood, soon passed away, and he found other friends among the black folks who worked with him in the fields.

Among them was a little boy of about his own age, who had somehow escaped being sold to the South. He was very black, but very bright; and though a poor slave child, with no friend in all the world but

his slave mother, he had a heart so light and happy
that he made everybody about him almost as happy
as he was. The two boys slept together in the same
cabin, and worked together in the same field, and
soon became as fast friends as were David and
Jonathan.

And so three years went away, and the annual sale
of young immortals left the two boys, Joseph and
Robert, still at work on the old plantation.

One morning, about this time, and right in the
hoeing season, word was circulated through the quarters that all the slaves, old and young, were to have
a holiday, and to come up to the green in front
of the "great house" for a general jollification. It
was a strange event, and a strange time for it to happen; but all the negroes arrayed themselves in their
best, and, with cheerful faces and merry hearts, went
up to the mansion. The two boys, unsuspicious of
any wrong, were following the rest, when an old
negro, hobbling along beside them, said : —

"I say, you boys, I reckon dar 'm a cat in dis yere
meal-tub. Massa hain't ober loikely ter feast him
darkies right in de middle ob wuck-time. Dis chile
doan't keer, fur he 'm too ole ter fotch a bad dollar,
but ye young 'uns had better tuck yer legs off ter
de woods, and leff de jollyfiration go."

At this, the boys paused, and took counsel together. It could not be, they thought, that their master would be so base as to sell them under such pretences; but the old negro said he would; that he had lived with the white man seventy years, and knew him capable of any kind of meanness or deception. This inclined them to be wary; but duty, they thought, required they should obey their master, and so they went to the mansion.

The court-yard contained several acres, tastefully laid out, and bordered by a dense growth of flowering shrubs and currant-bushes; and among these bushes they quietly hid themselves until the "merry-making" began in true Virginia fashion.

About two hundred negroes, of both sexes and all ages, had gathered in little knots on the lawn, eagerly waiting the signal to engage in their usual holiday sports, when their master and the overseer came out of the mansion. Going among them, the white men ordered this one and the other off to the field, till less than fifty were left clustered about the court-yard. These were told to sit down on the grass, and to remain·quiet until they were wanted. This they did, and in half an hour several strange white men rode up to the house, and the "sport" of the day began. Then the faces, lately so radiant with

6

sunshine, became overshadowed with clouds and deluged with rain. It was a sad, sad time. For years these simple people had associated together, and now, without a word of warning, they were to be separated; parents from children, brothers from sisters, husbands from wives, to meet no more this side of heaven. It seems to me — and I have seen many such scenes — that all the misery which can be borne by weak human nature has been borne by the poor blacks at these slave-sales. Such things, thank God, are now gone by forever; but it may be well to once in a while recall them, for they remind us that the men who have been guilty of so great cruelty in the past must be kept in check, or they may do still greater wickedness in the future.

Watching their opportunity, the two boys after a while stole away to the woods, where they remained until nightfall. Robert had a mother, and he feared that she might have been sold; and it was with a heavy heart that he at last turned his steps towards the quarter. Joseph had no mother, but he sympathized fully with the feelings of Robert; and it was a great relief when the good woman met them at the door-way of the little cabin. She had not been sold, but "Aunt Ruth" and "Uncle Jake," Joseph's only remaining relatives, were already on their way to the far South.

Four more toilsome years went away, and the boys were nearly fifteen, before another large sale occurred; but every year a half-dozen or more poor people were disposed of privately.

Among them was a young girl on whom Joseph had cast such eyes as young men very naturally cast on young women. Her name was Deborah. She was not far from fifteen and was very beautiful, with comely features, and a bright, clear complexion. She was a servant at the mansion, and her intelligence and gentle disposition had won her the confidence and affection of all on the plantation. One day her master told one of the men-servants to accompany her to Winchester; and, mounted on the back of an ancient mule, they set out, not suspecting the real object of the journey. Arrived at Winchester, they sought out the man to whom Deborah was consigned. He proved to be a slave-trader, and — the poor girl never came back again.

This occurrence sank deep into the hearts of the two boys. They were only fifteen, but they determined to be free, — free if they had to walk over burning ploughshares, and make their home among the icebergs of the northern seas. Soon an event occurred which led them to put their resolution into immediate action.

Another great holiday, another great "jollyfira-tion," came to the slaves on the old plantation. Again all ages went up to the mansion, and this time Joseph and Robert were too much grown to hide away among the currant-bushes. With the other slaves they were ranged along the lawn, and offered to the inspection of the men-dealers. The trader's cross was already on the back of Robert and his mother, — they were sold, — when he paused be-before Joseph, and asked him his age.

"I don't know, sir," answered the boy.

"Don't know!" exclaimed the trader; "this boy is a fool!" and he passed on, much to the boy's re-lief. Once before he had been let off because he was "too smart"; now he escaped because he was a fool; and the same man was the judge in both cases.

But the boy did not know how old he was. Scarcely any slave does know. He was born in the "dog-days," or at the first snow-fall; and he died at Christmas, or "a month after New-Year"; and that, written on the rude stake which marks his grave, is the whole of the slave's history.

But Robert and his mother were sold, and that was a sad night at the little cabin.

They were to set out on the following morning

for Richmond, New Orleans, or some other slave market, there to be again sold, and, no doubt, separated forever.

The prospect was appalling to the wretched mother; but she cared less about it for herself than for her son. Whatever became of herself, she wanted him to be free; and as she sat that evening by the meagre hearth, stirring silently the embers of the low fire, which, like her own hopes, was fast going out in the darkness, she turned suddenly to Robert, and said: "Run, Robby! Go ter-night, — ter onst. Keep de North Star right afore you, and travel on till you come ter freedom!"

For a moment Robert, too, sat gazing vacantly into the fire, but then he looked up, and answered, "Joe and I hab planned ter go, mother; but we'll not stir a step widout you."

"I can't go. I'm too old. I has rheumatiz. I could n't walk four mile a day. You'd only be kotched wid me along!" groaned the poor woman, rocking her body back and forth in her grief.

"Wall; if we is kotched we'll be no wuss off. We won't go widout you," now said Joseph.

This decided her, and she at once set about preparing for the dangerous journey. What surplus food was in her own and the adjoining cabins — for

the other blacks were let into the secret — was soon
collected in two small bundles ; and, about midnight,
they all sat down by the cheerless hearth, to wait till
the moon should set, and they could go off in safety.

Every night for six long years the boys had sat
there ; and every night, during all of that time, they
had gone to sleep on the narrow cot in the corner ;
but, whether the tranquil stars were telling of the
peace and joy of heaven, or the wailing storm was
echoing the unrest and sorrow of the earth, they
had never lain down without a dark shadow settling
about them, shutting out the green fields, and the
blue skies, and the golden-tinted clouds which color
the dreams of other boys, and leaving in sight only
the narrow pallet, the wretched hut, and the sweat-
sprinkled fields of the old plantation. But that night
their spirits rose from out the shadow ; and, though
thick clouds were shrouding all the sky, they saw the
stars shining ; and one star — to our eyes only a little speck, twinkling away in the Northern heavens —
come out, and grow, hour by hour, till it seemed a
great sun sent to light them on their journey. Years
rolled away as the boys looked, and they became
men, with strength to endure any hardship and over-
come any obstacle that might be in their way to
freedom.

In the midst of their reverie a rap came at the rickety door, and a low voice said : " Ho ! in dar ! You — brack folks ! "

Rising, Joseph undid the rude fastening, and let in the old man — Uncle David — who, years before, had warned the boys away from the great "jollyfira- tion." Helping him to settle himself upon a rude bench beside the hearth, Joseph said : " It 'm late fur you ter be round, Uncle Dave. What 'm done broke now ? "

" Nuffin 's done broke," answered the old negro ; " but suffin 'ould be mighty sudden, ef old Dave had n't a come ; b'case you 's a gwine off widout eber axin' him, when he know. ebery crook and turn ob dat road, jess like he 'd a trabelled it all his life."

" And why did n't you eber trabel it, Uncle ? " asked Robert's mother.

" 'Case de ole 'ooman lub de Missus, and would n't go ; but young Dave he went 'fore you was born, and arter he bought hisseff and git inter big business down dar in Baltimore, he holped a heap ob pore folks ober dat ar road ; and he 'll holp you ; and dat 's what I 'se come ter tell you 'bout."

" But we hain't a gwine ter Baltimore," said the boys. " We 'se a gwine stret up Norf."

" And dat 's jess how you 'll be took, and brung

back, and sole whar you 'll neber git away agin. Massa 'll be shore ter foller on de stret road. You muss lay low at de ole cabin on de mount'in till dey 'm off on de hunt; den you take de Norf star ober your leff shoulder, and put fur Baltimore. Go ter Dave, — ony brack folks 'll tell you whar he am, — and he 'll fix you de ress ob de way."

They thanked the old man; and, as he passed out of the low doorway, he put his hands on the heads of the boys, and asked Him who is the Father of the fatherless to be their guide and protector. Not long afterwards, they silently unbarred the door again, and stole out into the darkness.

PART II.

ON THE WAY TO FREEDOM.

THE plantation was on the western slope of the Blue Ridge, and, changing their route when they entered the forest, the fugitives climbed the long ascent, and made their way to a deep ravine which indents the eastern side of the mountain. In this ravine, hidden by a thick growth of pines and cedars, was the "ole cabin" to which "Uncle David" had alluded.

It was a wild, secluded spot, seldom, if ever, visited by a white man. About a year before, the two boys had discovered it, when rambling over the mountain on a Sunday; and its existence becoming known to the other slaves, it had been the refuge of the few who, since then, had staked their lives in a race with the dogs of their master. Shut in by high rocks and mountain-pines, and approached only by a shallow brook, which drowned the traces of footsteps, and balked the scent of bloodhounds, it was a spot where the runaway could lie for months as secure as if buried chin-deep amid the snows of Canada.

6 *   I

The hut was a rude structure of stones, roughly laid up in the mud of the stream; and it looked, overgrown as it was with moss and lichens, as if it had stood there since the antediluvian ages; but old David, who knew everything, — when it had once been told him, — insisted that it was built by one of his master's slaves, who ran away when he was a boy, and never afterwards was seen or heard of, — except now and then of a dark night when some late-stirring negro caught a glimpse of his ghost issuing from the smoke-house with a juicy ham or a brace of fat pullets over his shoulder. This could hardly be; for though the invisible gentry are accused of overturning chairs and tipping tables, it cannot be supposed that any ghost — even a black one — ever descended to the robbing of hen-roosts and smoke-houses. But, whether old David was right or wrong, it was certain that a human skeleton, its bones bleached to a snowy whiteness, and its clothing rotted away to the merest tinder, was found extended on the floor of the strange cabin when it was first discovered.

Into this cabin, just as the sun was saying "Good morning" to the world, the fugitives entered. The food they had brought, if carefully husbanded, would last them a week; and so they determined to remain there a couple of days ; and by that time they hoped their pursuers would be far away in a wrong direction.

Having decided on this delay, they sat down under a tree, and were watching the sun as it rose slowly above the mountain, when they heard the cry of dogs in the distance. Moving silently into the cabin, they waited. Swiftly it came on, — the yell of hounds and the shouts of men, — till it sounded directly over their heads ; a shrill, terrible cry, like the peal of the bell which summons the condemned man forth to his funeral. The woman sank to her knees, her hands clasped together, and her lips moving in mute supplication ; and the boys stood like statues, their teeth clenched, and their ears strained to catch the lightest sound which should come from the ravine below them.

They were not long in waiting. Soon the dogs reached the spot where the fugitives had struck the stream in their ascent to the cabin. Halting there, the fierce beasts sent up cry after cry, which rang through the deep wood, till even the still leaves seemed to tremble with terror. Erelong the voices of men mingled with the cry of the dogs, and then came the crisis in the lives of the dark people. The hounds had lost the scent in the water ; the men knew it, and were deliberating whether to follow up or down the little rivulet. If they went up, the fugitives were lost; if down, their way might yet be clear to freedom. The boys listened, and heard the words which were spoken. There were three of them, — their master, his brother, and the overseer. The latter thought the fugitives had gone up the ravine, but the others said, "No. The boys are smart and fleet-footed. They have taken to the water; but they'll make as many miles as they can before dark. If we follow down the run, the hounds will catch the trail again in half an hour."

They went down; but the danger was not yet over. The pursuers might return, and discover the cabin before nightfall. The fugitives feared this, and throwing their little bundles over their shoulders, they silently waded farther up the stream into the winding ravine. As they went, the rippling rivulet dwindled to a slender thread, scarcely covering the stones in its bed, and leaving their footprints plainly visible in the yielding sand. It would not do to go farther, for only running water will wash away the trace of human feet, and hounds will scent a single tread made on dry ground. A clump of small cedars was growing near the edge of the stream, and among them they would secrete themselves; but how to hide the traces of their footsteps was the question. Danger sharpens invention, and — whatever may be said to the contrary — the black brain is as fertile as the white one. They made a bridge of loose stones ; Robert and his mother passed over it ; and Joseph, following, carefully took up every stone, and threw it back into the rivulet.

The sun turned downward in the heavens, and the night came slowly on, — too slowly for the hunted people crouching amid the cedars, — until the shadows deepened along the dark ravine, and the stunted pines, standing among the gray rocks, looked like giant men, brandishing their arms against the murky sky, and about to close down on the poor fugitives. There was terror in the sight, but a greater terror in the sounds which now came faintly up from the foot of the mountain. It was the cry of the hounds returning, balked in the pursuit, and thirsting for the blood of these trembling people.

Slowly it came up, as if the men were with the dogs, and, wearied with the fruitless chase, were every now and then halting by the way. At last it ceased near the spot where the fugitives had taken to the water; and then it broke out again in hollow echoes, — winding up along the stream, towards the old cabin ! Soon it burst forth into

fierce yells, which broke the stillness of the dark
night, and smote on the hearts of the hunted people
like the strokes of a hammer on a blacksmith's anvil.
The men had discovered the hut, and the hounds
had scented the fugitives! The boys bent forward
to catch the words that were spoken; and the woman
sank to her knees, and stretched out her arms to
the great Father. A jutting rock hid the cabin from
their view; but the boys saw the torches, and heard
the talk of their pursuers.

"Some runaway built this," said the master, "and
perhaps lived here, feeding on my hen-roosts."

"And they have been here, all of them," cried
the overseer. "Here are their tracks, made since
sun-up! The hounds know it, and that is the reason they make such a howling."

"Let us go up the run," rejoined the master.
"They may have hidden farther up the ravine."

Then the red torches stole from behind the black
rock, and came towards the little clump of cedars.
The boys no longer held their breath, but the woman kept on with her praying.

"You mought as well stop," said Joseph. "De
Lord don't yere you. We am gone up; dat am
sartin!"

But the woman heeded him not. Still she kept

on her knees ; and still she stretched out her arms to the great Father.

The hounds were quiet, for they had again lost the trail, and the men paused, scarcely a hundred paces below the fugitives, and lifting their torches high in the air, looked narrowly round in the darkness. At last the master spoke : " They are not here," he said ; "and if they were, I would n't risk breaking my neck over these rocks for all the niggers in creation."

Then they turned, and went down the ravine ; and the woman's prayer changed to a low thanksgiving. Rising from her knees she said to the boys, " It am de Lord's doin's. *He* hab saved us from our enemies, — from de hand ob dem dat hate us." And every man and woman, from whose souls a true prayer has ever risen, knows that she spoke truly.

That night they lay down on the rough floor of the cabin, and slept soundly. In the morning, before the sun had thrust his head above the trees which fringe the top of the mountain, they heard the baying of hounds far away on the route, which, but for Old David, they would have taken.

" Shank's mares am de mares fur us now," cried Joseph, springing to his feet ; "and de sooner we 's stirrin' de better."

The woman tied her stout brogans over her shoulder, — the boys wore untanned "leathers," warranted to last a lifetime, — and they began the descent of the ravine, walking along the bed of the stream until the water grew too deep to wade in. Then they struck directly into the woods, keeping the sun all the while in their faces. They walked on for several hours, when they came to a cleared field, near which they paused, and hid themselves in a cedar thicket.

For four days they journeyed thus, in the woods by day, and in the road by night, until, near the close of the fourth day, they came to a hill from which they could see the steeples of Baltimore.

· Crouching behind some large trees near the highway, they waited there for the darkness. Slowly it came down, the blessed night, — so blessed to the weary worker and the hunted fugitive, — and the shadows deepened until the great trees looked like a regiment of black soldiers standing guard over the silent cornfields. Then they took to the highway, hoping to be soon safely housed with the black Christian of Baltimore.

They had not gone far before they heard wheels creeping along the road behind them. Hiding in a bend of the fence they waited. It was an old man, an old horse, and an old wagon, carrying a load of vegetables to market. When he came abreast of where they were, they saw that the man was black; and that assured them of aid and friendship. Stepping out from the shadow of the fence, Joseph accosted the traveller. "Aunty yere am all beat out, Uncle; she can't hardly walk no furder. Will you gub her a lift ter de city?"

"And who am you?" asked the negro, scanning them as closely as he could in the darkness.

Joseph stepped back a few paces, as he answered, "Jess what you am, — brack people dat hab wuckd der bery lives out fur de white folks."

"Yas," answered the old man; "and now you's runnin' away, — runnin' right inter de jaws ob de Philistin's! Why, honey, you won't sot foot in Baltimore, 'fore you'll be shot inter de lock-up, jess loike you wus stray critters dey cotch runnin' loose in de streets. Who does you know dar?"

"No un but young Dave, — Dave Pegram, what come frum Charlestown way."

"I knows. I knows. And you call *him* young!" exclaimed the old man, laughing. "Why, he'm older dan I is, ony day ob de week."

"But he'm young, dough," said Joseph, earnestly; "younger dan his fader."

"Well, you'm a smart chile, ter tink a son

younger dan his fader! But, hurry up. I can't be stayin' yere in de road,—some one 'll be comin' along. Leff de ole 'ooman git in under de punkins, —I 'll sell her fur one ef she don't keep quiet,—and you put across de field ter de fuss shanty. Stay dar till you yeres de Baltimore bells soundin' fur nine; den you follow you' noses ter de market;—you 'll find it by de smell. I 'll tote de ole 'ooman ter ole Dave's, and he 'll be dar waitin' fur you. Ef you come onter ary one in de streets dat eye you suspicious loike, you jess say you b'longs ter Squire Daniels, and am come in arter ole Jake, down ter de market. Ebery one know me, and dey 'll b'lieve what I says,—'case I neber lies, neber,—'cept now and den, jess ter keep my hand in."

The boys did as they were bidden; and at ten o'clock that night were accosted in the market-place by the sable Moses who led stray black children out of the wilderness. He took them to his own house, and concealed them for nearly a week. Then, with money furnished them by this true Israelite, they started on the journey northward.

Now they set the North Star directly before their faces. A few hours after noon of a pleasant day in July, they left Baltimore in a market-wagon, and were driven openly to the house of a planter living some

twelve miles from the city. They thought it strange
·they were thus consigned to the tender mercies of
a slaveholder; and had not "Young David" been
the son of his father, would have suspected him of
treachery. As it was, their minds were greatly disturbed when, halting at the doorway of the planter's
house, they were pointed out by him to another gentleman as "a prime lot," which he had just bought
in Baltimore. Robert was about to protest that this
was not true, when his mother checked him, and
whispered in the boy's ear, "Ef he 'm our friend, he
hab ter say dat ter make de ting luck clar ter de
gemman; ef he haint our friend, we can't holp our-
selfs. We must trust in de Lord."

They were taken to a neighboring cabin, and given
a hearty supper by an old negress who was in attend-
ance. After the meal was over she said to them:
"Now, chillen, you muss lay down and get all de
sleep you kin, 'case you 'se a long way afore you,
and you won't get off till nigh onter midnight."

"And den you' massa 'll holp us on ter de Norf,
jess loike Young David say he would!" said Joseph,
greatly reassured by the words of the woman.

"Ob course he will," answered the negress. "Massa hab bought more 'n twenty folks widin de year,
jess loike he buy you, ha! ha! and hab sole 'em

agin, way up Norf. He 'm one o' de directors ob
de underground railroad, — one ob de biggest on
'em. He make a heap in de business ; and he 'm
a layin' it all up — up dar — whar de moth doan't
eat, and de tief doan't steal, and by de time he come
ter die, I reckon he 'll hab such a pile in de Lord's
han's, dat nuffin but de interest on it will leff him
lib loike a gemman foreber."

"He must be a good man ; but — haint he a
slaveholder?" asked Joseph hesitatingly.

"Ob course he am ; dat 's how he kin holp you ;
fur nobody wud 'spect *him* ob doin' what he do fur
de hunted ones. He hab eighteen ; but we all
knows de free papers am made out agin he die ;
and nary one on us wud leab him, not ter lib wid
Garrison hisseff."

After a few hours sleep the fugitives were put into
a covered wagon, with a negro driver, and driven off
towards Pennsylvania. The horses were fleet, and
an hour before daybreak set them down at a house
in the outskirts of the little town of Gettysburg ;
where, since then, a great battle has been fought on
which hung the fate of the nation.

It was an old house, clad in a coat of faded gray ;
and a huge sign swinging before its door told that
it was a tavern. The driver tapped three times on

one of the lower windows, and soon a side-door
opened, and an old man, in a night-cap and a dress-
ing-gown, came out into the moonlight. He greeted
the driver cordially, and ushered the fugitives into
a small room on the ground-floor adjoining the kitch-
en. Asking them to be seated, he lit a candle, and
gave them a look of close scrutiny.

"Aha!" he said, turning his eyes from them to
a printed handbill above the mantel-piece. "Here
you are, and your master asleep in the room over-
head! Now, I could make five hundred dollars so
quick it would make your heads swim!"

Robert's mother sank to her knees; but the boys
sprang to their feet, and, with flashing eyes, cried
out: "Der yer mean ter betray us?"

"Hush, you fools," said the man, "or he'll hear
you. He came here a week ago, and has been.
scouring all Pennsylvania. He returned last night,
and will go back after breakfast; then you'll be
safe for a short century; for he thinks you're hid
somewhere in Baltimore. Don't stir from this room;
keep the door locked, and don't even look out of the
windows. At night I'll send you on to the next
station."

It was a long day to the fugitives, but it came
to an end at last; and, about an hour after dark,

they set out again towards the North Star, which once more, like a sun, lighted their way to freedom. For two nights they journeyed, and just at sunrise, on the morning of the second day, halted at a farm-house in the edge of Clinton County. There they were washing their faces at a little spring, and brushing off the dust of the journey, when a young girl came rushing from the house, and, throwing her arms about Joseph's neck, almost devoured him with kisses.

It was Deborah! The trader had sold her to a planter near to Winchester; and, after a year's service, she had escaped, and, aided by the good "underground" people, had found a quiet home among the hills of Pennsylvania. She begged her master to give Joseph work, and he did so; paying him five dollars a month and his clothing. He also secured employment for Robert and his mother on a farm in the neighborhood; and so the fugitives found freedom, and knew the blessing of working for wages.

PART III.

FREEDOM.

ABOUT thirty negro men — one half of them escaped slaves — were working on farms within a circuit of three or four miles of the one on which Joseph had found employment. These men had formed among themselves a combination which they called the "Defensive League," with the object of preventing the legal arrest of any of their number under the Fugitive Slave Law, or their illegal capture by any of the bands of kidnappers who now and then entered the district, and, without warrant or the pretence of authority, tore fugitives, and sometimes free colored men from their beds at dead of night, and bore them into hopeless slavery across the border. Every member of the League was furnished with a rifle and a hunting-knife, and was at liberty to use, in case of need, the horse of his employer, or of some neighboring farmer. They acted strictly on the defensive; but, within a fortnight of our fugitives coming into the district, had rescued a colored woman from the clutches of the men-stealers, and, during the previous five years, had done

similar service to many a hunted runaway. With
their first earnings, Robert and Joseph procured the
necessary weapons, and then joined this organization.

Everything went on quietly for a year, and the
new garments of freedom were beginning to sit easily
on the growing limbs of the two boys, when, late
one night, Joseph was roused from sleep by a heavy
pounding on his master's window. Thrusting his
head out, he saw a woman, — the wife of the farmer
with whom Robert was working. Listening, he heard
her say, " I stole away before they got into his
room ; but there are three of them, and they have
him half-way to the Haven by this time."

He waited for no more ; but, throwing on his coat
and trousers, seized his rifle, and rushed to the barn
for one of his master's horses. Taking the fleetest
animal in the stable, he galloped down the road the
kidnappers were supposed to have taken, stopping
only to rouse such of his confederates as lived on
the route. In half an hour four had joined him,
and with them he rode rapidly on to the village of
Lock Haven.

The party had ridden two hours, seeing no one,
and getting no trace of the kidnappers, when they
entered the village, and halted at its only tavern

The door was ajar, and a dim light was burning in the bar-room. Springing from his horse, Joseph questioned the sleepy hostler. "Yes, I 've seed 'em," said the man. "They stopped here for drinks, — two on horses, and one with the darky, tied in a wagon. They 've tuck the stret road; but yer three miles ahind of them."

"Three miles am nuffin," shouted Joseph, bounding into his saddle. "De drinks hab saved Robert."

In an hour they caught up with the kidnappers. The wagon drove rapidly on, while the horsemen made a stand in the road; but eluding them, Joseph dashed after the fleeing vehicle. In twenty minutes he caught up with it, and, dealing the driver a blow which stretched him senseless on the ground, he undid Robert's bonds, and, mounting him on the back of his horse, rode off, by a circuitous route, homewards. Meanwhile the other kidnappers had made a brave defence, and were not overpowered until one of them was mortally wounded. He was taken to the nearest house, and there died at noon of the following day. This unfortunate occurrence caused a great huc-and-cry, and led to the arrest of many of the black men in the neighborhood. Suspicion naturally pointed to Joseph, and he escaped the officers only by the help of friends and the greatest vigi-

lance. So it was that, with Robert and Dinah,—
Robert's mother,— he again became a fugitive.

Where should they go? Canada was too cold;
and the men-stealers, they were told, patrolled every
rural district of New York and Pennsylvania. They
would seek a great city, and among a multitude of
strangers hope to find safety. Taking a letter to a
worthy Quaker, they set out one night for Philadelphia.

The Quaker received them cordially, procured
them quiet lodgings, gave Joseph work in his own
store, and secured Robert employment with a neigh-
bor. Dinah took in washing, besides keeping house
for the boys; and it was not long, with their united
economy and industry, before they had a snug little
sum on deposit in a savings-bank.

But Joseph was not happy. He looked back with
regret to the smaller wages and harder work of the
little farm in Clinton County. "Why is this?" he
asked himself; as he set about a quiet inspection
of his internal mechanism.

All at once it flashed upon him that Deborah was
not with him! She it was who had made the farm-
work light, and the farmer's silver dollars outweigh
the Quaker's golden eagles! That night he went
to the worthy Quaker, and the result of an hour's

conversation was the following letter, written by the latter, to Deborah.

"DEAR DEBORAH : —

"Thee is young, — so am I. Thee is poor, — so am I. Thee is all alone in the world, — so am I. But thee won't be poor, nor all alone, nor always young, — for we'll grow old together, — if thee will become my wife. The old Quaker that I work for, and who pays me thirty dollars a month, has put ten dollars into this letter to buy thee a wedding-gown, and to pay thy passage to thy affectionate

"JOSEPH.

"P. S. — Come at once. Don't thee* wait for the · gown. Calico is cheap in Philadelphia."

She came at once, and had the wedding-gown, all of silk, on the wedding-day.

Then a year went away, the happiest year that Joseph and Deborah had ever known. In their snug little room up four pair of stairs they looked down with a feeling akin to pity on the gaudily-dressed ladies and gentlemen who rolled along in gilded carriages below them. And well they might; for were they not exactly four stories nearer heaven than those white people?

But the war broke out. Fort Sumter fell; and a great storm arose in the North, stirring even the quiet atmosphere of that little room in the fourth story. Joseph grew silent and abstracted; some earnest thought was working within him, driving smiles from his face and slumber from his eyelids. One night, when Dinah and Deborah were clearing away the tea-things, he turned abruptly to Robert, who had seated himself to his evening lesson in the spelling-book, and said: "Rob, ef I goes ter de war, and gits killed, will you marry Deborah?"

"Marry Deborah!" exclaimed Robert; and "Marry me!" echoed Deborah. "I reckon it 'll tuck two ter make dat bargain."

"Yes," answered Joseph, "it 'll tuck *three*, — Rob, and you and *me!* What does ye say, Rob? Is ye willin'?"

"Ob course I is," laughed Robert. "But what do de gal say ter dat?"

"She haint a willin', and you sha' n't go," said Deborah, throwing her arms about the neck of Joseph.

"You need n't fear 'bout dat," said Robert; "he carn't go. I knows, 'case I 'se axed de sodger round de corner. He say dey won't tuck no folks dat am brack in de face."

"Not fur sodgers," answered Joseph; "but I 'se seed a Cap'n ob de Ninfh New York, dat say he 'll tuck me along as his servant, and guv me a chance ter handle a musket when dey comes on ter de Secesh."

This put a more serious aspect upon the matter; and while Deborah hung more closely about Joseph's neck, old Dinah said: "But ye carn't mean ter go, —ter leab firty dollar a month, and a kind master, ter wuck fur only firteen, and a gubment as doan't keer de price ob a sorry nigger fur all de brack folks in de worle!"

"Well, massa say I orter. He say he 'd go ef he was only ob my color," replied Joseph.

"Den he 'm a ole hyppercrit," said Deborah, "'case all dem Quaker folks preach up non-resistunce."

"Dat 's what massa say," answered Joseph; "but he say dat ar doctrine warn't meant fur dese times. In dese times, he say, ebery man ob my color orter shoulder a musket."

And so, Joseph went to the war, and was one of those twenty thousand men, who, with the doughty Patterson, "marched up a hill, and then — marched down again."

The army had been marching and countermarch-

ing through the mud and dust of Virginia for many
weeks, when, at the close of a hot day in July, 1861,
it came in sight of the steeples of Charlestown.
This was Joseph's early home, and the spot where
was builded a gallows for that brave old man whose
soul, these four years, has "been marching on," carrying terror to every slaveholder from the Potomac
to the Rio Grande. The town was the very hot-bed
of Secession, and, when our army entered it, singing,

> "John Brown's body lies a-mouldering in the grave,
>   But his soul is a-marching on,"

every door was closed, every window curtained, and
every street as deserted and silent as a graveyard.

But with the morning a change came over the
spirit of its dream. The blacks, who had somehow
discovered they were not to be sold to Cuba, or
burned as back-logs by the Northern men, came
timidly from their hiding-places, and gazed idly on
the strange spectacle ; and the whites unbarred their
doors, and, with a leg of greasy bacon under one
arm, and a pot of muddy coffee, or a loaf of soggy
corn-bread under the other, sallied forth, and charged
boldly on the Yankee soldiers, intent on capturing
their Yankee gold.

The soldiers bought freely ; and, far and near, the

news travelled, until, at last, it reached the ear of Joseph's former master; and then followed such a baking of pies and brewing of beer as was never known on the old plantation. The master was too old, or too cowardly, to meet the Yankees in the open field, with an honest rifle; but he determined to waylay them in the crowded street, and with leaden pastry strike them such heavy blows — in the stomach — as would prove more fatal than a braver man's leaden bullets. He was one of the Chivalry; and so you may think that he would not so far forget his own dignity, and the pride of his class, as to indulge in the peddling propensities of the Yankees; but if you think this, you do not know the Chivalry. I know them, and I never knew one of them who, in this kind of warfare, was not the equal of any five Yankees in the world.

Well, the planter determined to scatter death among the invaders; so he got out the old market-wagon, filled it with stale hams, unripe fruit, and pastry heavy enough to sit hard on even his conscience; and then, with old David as driver, set out for Charlestown. Entering the village not far from sunset, he directed his steps at once to the spot where the largest number of people were gathered. This happened to be a street-corner, where a

Union soldier, mounted on a barrel, was holding forth to a motley collection of whites and negroes on the inestimable blessings of freedom, — how it was a good thing for the white man, and would not do any sort of harm to the black one. At the close of one of his finest periods, the wagon came to a halt, and old David sung out: "Dat am all so, gemman and ladies; but yere am yer fine fresh pie, yer nice, juicy ham, and yer boilin' hot coffee. So walk up, walk up, gemman and l-a-d-i-e-s. Only s-e-v-e-n-t-y-f-i-v-e cents for a slice ob ham, a cup ob coffee, and a piece ob pie what wa'n't made o' shoe-leather."

The orator was at the beginning of another glowing sentence; but he turned abruptly on the old negro, and called out, "Shut up, you old fool; take your apple-cart somewhere else."

"And dat 'm de sort ob freedom you 'se come down yere ter talk 'bout!" responded old David, grinning very widely. "I reckons I haint lib'd yere fur sebenty year, widout findin' out dat dat haint no freedom ter preach in dese diggin's."

"Go it, old man!" "Give it to him, Yankee!" "Hustle him out!" and a score of similar exclamations arose from the crowd, which now swarmed round the wagon, like an army of flies round a molasses hogshead, threatening to devour its sweets without paying the revenue officer. The keen eye of the old darky saw the danger; and, mounting upon the top of the pile, he laid about with his whip in a way that kept both friends and enemies at a distance. At last his lash, unluckily, came in contact with a soldier's profile. This was more than the freeman could bear, and, with a blow on the old man's breast, he sent him sprawling into the middle of the street.

The planter, meanwhile, had slunk away into the crowd, leaving his load of eatables and his faithful old servant to their fate; and there is no telling what that fate might have been, had not a new actor appeared on the scene. It was Joseph. Seizing the soldier by the collar, and tossing him over the wheels of the wagon as if he had been a bag of feathers, he planted himself above the prostrate old man, and cried out to the now half-riotous crowd, "Come on! you cowards, dat tackle a ole man loike dis. Come on! and I 'll guv you a lesson in freedom dat 's wuth larnin'."

No one seeming disposed to come on, the old darky, rising to his feet, added his invitation. "Yas, come on!" he cried. "One Suddern man kin whip five Yankees, and two kin whip twenty. We am Suddern men, so you come on!"

This ridiculous challenge restored the good-nature

7 *

of the assemblage; and, after old David had sufficiently hugged his unexpected deliverer, they "come
on," and emptied the planter's wagon, leaving in the
hands of Joseph, who acted as "sub-treasurer" and
"money-changer," a larger quantity of "current coin"
than could then be found in the vault of any bank
in the "Old Dominion."

In this altered condition of affairs, the planter
emerged from the mass of people, and came toward
Joseph, with a face as smiling as an April day after
a shower. "Ah, Joseph!" he said, "I am glad to
see you back, — glad to see you again serving your
old master!"

Joseph drew himself up with all the dignity of
an exalted functionary receiving some cringing sup-
plicant for office, and answered: "And who am
you, sah?"

"Why, I'm your old master!" replied the planter,
with a look of blank amazement.

"My massa, sah!" exclaimed "the property," "I
haint no massa 'cept Uncle Sam, as you kin see by
my clo'es, — and you! Now I 'member you, —
you'se one o' dem ole Secesh what hung John Brown,
and we'se come out yere ter hang *you*, — 'spressly
ter do dat, sah!"

The planter was now half petrified with astonish-

ment ; but he faltered out in a conciliatory tone :
"Old friends should n't quarrel, Joseph. I make no
claim to you. You have earned your freedom."

At this the dignity of the "chattel" suddenly for-.
sook him, and bending forward he whispered in the
ear of his master : "Make out de free papers den, —
make 'm out ter night; and den you 'll sabe you'
neck, and git you' money"; and he coolly placed
the bag of specie in the breast of his coat.

The planter watched the vanishing bag as the
British bondholders may be supposed to have watched
the falling Confederate loan, — going down inch by
inch, till it sunk at last with a sudden plunge, fully
out of sight; but he coolly said, "Well, I will.
Come to the plantation to-night, at nine o'clock, and
the papers shall be ready."

"No, sah!" said Joseph, "you don't cotch ole
birds wid salt! You come ter *me*, — ter de camp ob
de Ninfh New York, — dat 's de rigimen' I b'longs
ter!"

"Well, I will," answered his master. "At nine
o'clock, — you 'll be there?"

"I 'll be dar!" answered the colored gentleman,
walking away with the dignified strut of a New York
alderman, who has just thrust his hand into the
"public crib," and — is proud of the achievement.

In much the same mood, he was, about nine o'clock that night, pacing the grass in front of his Captain's tent, when his master and another gentleman approached him. The latter wore a blue uniform, and Joseph saw, at a glance, was the Provost-Marshal of the army. What could the officer be doing with his master? But Joseph was not long in doubt about his errand.

"That is the boy!" said the planter, pointing to his property, without giving it even a look of recognition.

"Come with me, boy," said the Marshal, laying his hand on Joseph's shoulder.

"'Scuse me, sah," answered Joseph with considerable of his recent dignity, — for so much could not be expected to evaporate in a moment. "I 'se engaged wid de Cap'n."

"Never mind the Captain; come with me," said the officer.

"I t'anks you, sah! I 'd rudder nut," answered Joseph, stepping back towards the door of the tent.

The Captain, who had listened to this conversation from the inside of the tent, now came out, and said to the Marshal, "Major, what does this mean? What do you want with Joseph?"

"He is claimed by this gentleman as his slave,"

said the officer ; "and the General's orders are to harbor no runaways."

"But Joseph is not a runaway. I got him in Philadelphia. What evidence have you that he ever belonged to this man ?"

" Heaps of evidence," cried the planter, in an excited tone. "My word, sir! I tell you he is my property, and has stolen a bag of my money. He has it now about him."

"You lie, you ole debble," shouted Joseph, drawing out the bag, and launching it at the head of the planter. "I haint got you' money !"

According to rule, Joseph "aimed low," and missing his face, the bag struck the master in the region of his pocket. The blow brought him down, and at the same time loosened the fastening of the bag, and scattered the coin, in a silver shower, all over the ground. Rising soon to his knees, the planter groped about for his runaway dollars, apparently forgetful of his other runaway property, which, even then, was not of much value for "general circulation" in Virginia.

While the planter was searching for his stray gold, the Captain and the Provost-Marshal continued the conversation. The former declined to give up the fugitive without express orders from the General;

but, it being too late to obtain access to that officer that evening, he at last consented to Joseph's being lodged over night in jail, to await his decision in the morning. So, in half an hour, the slave lad found himself a tenant of the little cell from which John Brown went forth to die on the scaffold.

His reflections, when the great key turned in the lock, and he was left alone in the gloomy room, were, as you may imagine, not of a very cheerful character. He thought of Deborah, of Robert, and of Robert's mother, from all whom he soon would be separated forever; he thought of the far South, of its hot sugar-fields, and deadly rice-swamps, to which he would be sold as soon as the army went away; and he thought of the faithless government, for which he had offered his life, and which was now plunging him again into the abyss of slavery. He thought of all this, for already he knew his fate. The Captain had whispered, as he bade him "Good night" at the door: "Get away, Joe, if you can, — it is your only chance. Old Patterson is a pro-slavery man, if not a traitor. I shall do all I can; but I have no hope. He will give you up."

"Get away? A camel may go through the eye of a needle; a rich man may go to heaven; but no human creature ever went through these prison-walls." So thought Joseph, as he looked round his gloomy cell, and laid down to rest on a bundle of straw in the corner.

In the morning a soldier came in with his breakfast. The man had a kindly face, and Joseph, drawing him into conversation, soon learned that he was from Massachusetts. "You did n't cum out yere ter stand guard ober runaway darkys, — shore!" said Joseph.

"Well, I did n't," answered the man. "I enlisted for another sort of work, — for freeing 'em. I 'd help you if I could; but I must obey orders. What do you mean to do?"

"Die, sooner dan go back ter slavery!"

"That 's the talk," responded the soldier, "and here 's a knife to help you. But, whatever happens, don't hurt *yourself*. Kill the men-stealers, — never kill yourself."

"Dar 's a gal up Norf would keep me frum doin' dat, anyhow," said Joseph, putting the weapon — which was half dirk, half butcher-knife — into the lining of his jacket. "Wid dis I 'll git my freedom!"

The soldier left him, and the hours wore slowly away until he came again with his dinner. The man's face wore a look of more than usual animation, and, closing the door carefully, he said: "Your Captain has just been here. He did all he could, but old Patterson has decided against you. The Captain says your master will no doubt come here within an hour; and he wants you to go with him peaceably; for to-night, with half a dozen men, he 'll kidnap you, and have you twenty miles away by morning. He 'll do it, if it costs him his commission."

Tears were in the slave boy's eyes as he sat down and ate his dinner in silence. He was not utterly forsaken; white men were not utterly false; some of them had yet hearts somewhere about their bodies. This feeling was uppermost in him, when, an hour or two later, he was summoned to meet his master.

The old man had come alone, with an open wagon. With the lieutenant of the guard, and half a dozen other soldiers, he was standing at the doorway of the jail as Joseph came out with the attendant. A look of grim satisfaction was on his face when he caught sight of he chattel; but it changed to an expression of serious concern as he noticed that neither his hands nor his feet were manacled. Turning to the soldiers, he said : " Here, give me a piece of rope. I 'm sure the General don't know you have n't tied the boy."

The General was high in favor with the slave-owner; and deservedly so. He had not only poured out loyal gold by the bushel in payment for Rebel crops,—which gold was at once converted into the sinews of Rebel war, — but had also allowed every kidnapper in Virginia free access to his camp in pursuit of runaways ; and thus afforded Johnson full information of the strength and probable movements of his army. History will be at no loss for the reason why Patterson, with "twenty thousand men, marched up a hill, and then marched down again."

The Lieutenant. gave no heed to the planter's request ; but one of the men threw him a piece of tent-rope, with which he attempted to tie Joseph's ankles together. But, strange as it may seem, the ankles objected to being tied! Only one of them could possibly be made to submit to the operation ; and, after tugging away at the other until he was out of breath and red in the face, the planter turned to the officer, and said, — a sickly smile playing round the corners of his sunken mouth, — "I say, Leftenant, just let one of your men lend me a hand to tie the boy's legs. He's durned lightfooted."

The officer was a Boston boy, and this was work he was not accustomed to. With great effort he had smothered his wrath until then ; but then it burst forth like a clap of thunder. "Begone, you infernal ruffian!" he cried. "Take your property, and be-

K

gone! If one of my men touches your rope, I'll give him what will make him hate rope as long as he lives. Begone, I say! Take your property, and begone!"

The planter had heard thunder before; but never any thunder that foretold such a storm as then was brewing. Hastily turning to Joseph, he said, in a whining, pleading tone: "Joseph — won't you — won't you — get into the wagon?"

Joseph could gain nothing by a refusal. He could not possibly escape in the midst of the camp, surrounded as he was by thousands bound to obey the orders of their General; so, releasing his ankle from the rope, he stepped nimbly into the wagon, and bade "Good by" to the soldiers. His master took a seat beside him, and applying the whip to the horse, drove rapidly away.

He drove down the broad street which runs through the centre of the town; but what was Joseph's consternation when, reaching the outskirts, he turned into a road leading directly away from the plantation! By a flash of thought, the slave lad took in "the situation." He was not going "home." He could not be liberated by the Captain! His master had already sold him, and was driving him away for "delivery." These thoughts flashed upon him, and his plan was formed in an instant. It involved an old man's life; but he would be free, if the lives of forty old men had to be sacrificed.

"Massa," he said coolly, "you 'se tuck de wrong road."

"I know which road I 've taken, boy," said the master; "we 've not far to go." And he put whip to his horse, and urged him on even more rapidly.

An ordinary meal-bag lay in the bottom of the wagon. What was in it Joseph did not know; but it evidently contained something which his master would not care to leave behind. When the planter's face was turned a trifle, Joseph touched the bag with his foot, and tossed it into the road, exclaiming, "Golly, massa, who 'd a tort sich a lettle kick as dat would a sent de bag ober. But you need n't neber mind; I 'll jess git out and hab it in a jiffin."

The master looked at him for a moment, then said: "No, I reckon not. I reckon, if you get out, you 'll take to your legs. I 'll get the bag myself."

Joseph's heart beat faster; a cold shudder passed over him; for by this ruse he had hoped to save his master's life, and now he saw him rushing blindly on his fate! The planter got out of the wagon, and with the reins backed the horse to where the bag lay in the highway. Then he threw it into the wagon, and was preparing to get in himself, when a happy thought struck Joseph, — a thought which no doubt saved the planter's life. The reins were in the planter's hand, and his hand was on the side of the wagon, when, quickly drawing his knife, Joseph severed them at a blow, and, springing up, applied the whip to the horse's back. The frightened animal bounded away, leaving the astonished planter standing in the middle of the road. His shouts and curses came down the wind, but they only struck fire from the horse's heels, and widened the distance between him and his property. On they went, over the stones, through the mud and the mire, till the poor animal could go no farther. Then Joseph halted, tied him to a tree by the roadside, and opened the meal-bag. In it were a revolver, a pair of handcuffs, and a flask of whiskey.

"Dese yere is contraband ob war," said Joseph to himself; "but I 'll jess be fa'r, and divide wid massa. I 'll leab him de bag, and de han'cuffs; and tuck de 'volver and de wiskey. If I doant, what wid his wrof, and de wiskey, he 'll kill hisseff wid de 'volver, jess ter releab his feelin's."

But he must have uttered this soliloquy as he walked forward; for he lost no time in plunging into the woods, and making his way into Pennsylvania.

It was two days before he reached a place of safety ; and, meanwhile, he lived upon the whiskey.

For nearly three years after these events he remained at home, working for the good Quaker, and happy with Deborah in the little room in the fourth story. Then he went to the war again.

The government had at last learned that the black man is a man, and had called upon him to assist in putting down the Rebellion. Joseph was among the first to respond to the call; and, leaving his bounty with Deborah, and exacting again from Robert the promise that he would marry her, in the event of his falling in battle, he enlisted as a private in the Thirty-first Regiment of United States Colored Infantry.

He was on his way to the front when I met him; and this is the story he told me while we sat, till the early hours of the morning, in the state-room of a little government steamer, going down the Potomac. I have not seen him since; and heard nothing about him till many months afterwards. Then, one day, I happened to be in Philadelphia, and, thinking of Joseph, I sought out the old Quaker.

He is known far and wide, and is a man with a heart as broad as the brim of his hat, and "a hand as open as day for melting charity." He told me that

Joseph was still living, and still in the army. In the attack on Petersburg, which occurred about a month after I met him, Joseph's regiment was engaged, and he was wounded. He was laid up for three months with his wound, but then rejoined his regiment, and was with it in all the great battles which followed. He was again wounded in one of the fights before Richmond, but remained with his command, and stood bravely by till the last blow was struck and the great Rebellion went down forever. For his good conduct and bravery he had been promoted to the rank of Sergeant.

Robert was working for the old Quaker, in the place of Joseph; and he and Dinah and Deborah were still living together; but no longer in a fourth story. They had come down at least twenty feet nearer the earth; and there, after dinner, the old Quaker and I called upon them. I found them living in great comfort; and Deborah showed me a little book which told that they had eleven hundred dollars on deposit in a savings-bank.

And here ends my story; and I hope it has shown you that black people are men and women, and entitled, as such, to all the blessings and privileges of freedom.

PRISON PICTURES.

JEFF DAVIS AS A PRISONER.

I WAS coming from the South, one day during the war, when I met an acquaintance on the railway, who said to me: "What a grand thing it would have been if you had captured Jeff Davis in Richmond, and brought him along in an iron cage, as Ney would have done with Napoleon! You might have made a fortune in the show business, and have crushed the Rebellion at a single blow, into the bargain."

"Do you think so?" I replied, with the air of a man who is conscious of having done something wonderful, and — is aching to tell about it. "Do you think Jeff Davis would draw good houses?"

"Good houses!" he exclaimed with enthusiasm. "He would pack Cooper Institute a hundred nights running, at a dollar a head."

"Then," I remarked, "I am tempted to go into the show business; for, to tell you the truth, I am out of pocket on him a considerable sum, and would like to be reimbursed."

8

"What do you mean?" asked my friend, his eyes dilating to an uncommon size. "What *do* you mean?"

"Simply what I say," I replied, in a tone which showed that my fancy was already jingling those dollars in my pocket. "I *have* caged Jeff Davis; got him safe under lock and key in a forward car."

My acquaintance seemed, for a time, stupid with astonishment; then, rising, he proposed that I should allow him a sight of my captive gratis, in advance of the rest of the world. I felt by instinct that he thought I was romancing; so I readily assented, and, staggering forward over the jolting train, soon gave him a view of the great Rebel through the car window.

He gazed at him long and earnestly, — as an art-critic gazes at a beautiful statue, or a jockey at a blooded animal, — then, turning to me, said: "He's a splendid fellow, — has the carriage of a king, 'an eye to threaten and command.' Why! he's fit to lead any army in Christendom!"

The gentleman was the least bit of a Secessionist; so I was not surprised at this exuberance of admiration, and merely remarked: "Isn't he wonderfully like his pictures?"

"Wonderfully!" he replied, adding, as he slapped

me familiarly on the shoulder, "Ah, my dear fellow, you have a prize; you're well paid for going to Richmond."

. We resumed our seats, and I pondered over the project my friend had suggested. We were leaving New York, and going towards Boston, and there-fore I could not act in the matter at once, even if I did resolve to turn showman; for no mammoth humbug ever originated in the "city of notions," — that is, none worth naming. New York gave birth to Barnum and the Woolly Horse; and on the metropolitan stage, if anywhere, Jeff Davis should make his first bow to "the million."

I had pretty well settled this in my mind, when we arrived at our journey's end, and stepped out upon the platform. I settled with the conductor for Jeff's fare; paying him forty-five dollars, all in greenbacks, — for you must know the aristocratic Rebel had a whole car to himself; and then set out for my home, a few miles from the city.

Jeff no sooner put foot on the sidewalk, than he lifted his head, and tossed his nose into the air, as if conscious that he was near the spot where Mr. Toombs proposed to call the roll of his colored children, and scorned the very ground he trod on. But, notwithstanding his high looks, he was, as my friend had observed, a "splendid fellow," — with clean, well-formed limbs, lithe, closely-knit frame, noble, regular features, and an eye in whose dark depths slumbered a thunderbolt.

He wore a snugly-fitting suit of black, — handsomer than any ever made by a Yankee tailor, — and made, altogether, an appearance not to be ashamed of; but I carefully avoided introducing him to my city friends, lest the receipts of the talked-of exhibition should be lessened. I did, however, present him to the editor of a Secession newspaper, who, a short while before, had assured me he was well acquainted with Jeff Davis, and knew him to be a perfect gentleman, — "Yes, sir, a *perfect* gentleman."

I naturally concluded that Jeff would be particularly glad to meet his Secession friend ; but, strange as it may appear, he did not seem to recognize him. In fact he turned up his nose at him, refusing to answer even a word, though the gentleman greeted him very cordially, and was profuse in his attentions. This satisfied me that great Rebels thoroughly despise small ones; and that Northern men, who do dirty work for the South, are liable to be paid with more kicks than coppers.

Then we started homewards. On the route Jeff

tried to get away, and acted very much as if he would
like to tread me underfoot; but I clung to him as
death is supposed to cling to a dead herring, and
finally got him safely to the door-way of the old
house by the cemetery.

The children knew we were coming; and all of
them came out to greet us. Jeff stood somewhat
upon his dignity, but behaved very well for one
of the chivalry. Not so some of our young folks.
"Billy Boy" whispered in the hearing of the captive, "Is dat de ole Reb, Deff Davis, dat you reads
about in de newspapers?" and his older brother answered: "Of course it is. Father's captured him,
down South. He says he's uglier'n Cain, and you
mus' n't go within a mile of him."

Having got the prisoner home, the next thing was
to lodge him where he could not get away, and
would be accessible at a moment's notice for the
possible exhibition. It would not do to take him
into the house with the family, for not a member of
it would sleep under the same roof with a Rebel.
But on "our farm of three acres" is an out-building
not large enough for a barn, and not small enough
for a stable, and with too little architectural ginger-
bread about it to pass for a pigeon-house. In that we
determined to confine his Southern Majesty. With

great care we fitted up for him a parlor and bedroom, and then ushered him into his domicile with great ceremony.

The accommodations were really very fine, and Jeff appeared perfectly satisfied with them; but I had no sooner turned my back upon him than, without any provocation, he came at me "tooth and nail," putting his huge "grinders" through my coat-sleeve and into my arm, as if he were a cannibal, and wanted me for an evening meal. Luckily, I know something of "the manly art of self-defence," so I let my fists fly into his face until it was black as a hat, and he relinquished his hold, thoroughly beaten. This was a most ungentlemanly proceeding on his part, and not a very dignified one on mine; but it was the best I could do in the circumstances.

Then he grew so furious that I scarcely dared to go near him; and the man I had hired as his special attendant utterly refused to set foot on the premises. I was deliberating what to do in this emergency, when "Billy Boy's" older brother — a little fellow of twelve — said to me: "Pshaw, father, there is n't any danger. *I'm* not afraid of him, if he is a big Rebel. I 'll give him his meals myself."

I was not anxious the boy should be eaten; so I watched his first entrance into his Majesty's domain with a good deal of solicitude, — standing by ready to rescue him in case of necessity. But my fears were groundless. Jeff shook hands with the boy, and treated him throughout the interview with the utmost politeness and affability. After that they grew very friendly together; never meeting without shaking hands, and caressing each other as if they were own brothers. But the big Rebel showed the same surly disposition to me; and I paid him off with rations which none of you would eat, — wholesome, but coarser and harder to digest than the wretched stuff dealt out to our poor boys at Salisbury and Andersonville.

About this time I came across the "Life of P. T. Barnum, written by Himself," and read it through from end to end. It contains, as you know, the instructive histories of Joice Heath, the Woolly Horse, and the Mermaid; and, if you ever read them, you will be at no loss for my reason for deciding not to play second fiddle to a showman, and not to adventure with my prize in the show business. So my great exhibition turned out a glass palace after all.

But what to do with Jeff Davis, was now the question. Notwithstanding his ugliness, it was cruel to keep him so closely confined, when his captivity seemed to have no effect whatever on the Rebellion.

This was in November, just prior to the Presidential election; and, while I was revolving the subject in my mind, several gentlemen rode up to the house, and invited me to make a political speech that evening at the Unitarian Church, where was to be a grand "powwow," — the brass band, Hail Columbia, Yankee Doodle, Star-Spangled Banner, Old John Brown, and the Big Fiddle. The gentleman who had agreed to address the meeting had been "Two Years before the Mast," and all round the world, without accident, but that day had been shipwrecked on a railway; and if I did not consent to make "a few remarks," "nothing would be said by nobody," — except the brass band and the Big Fiddle.

I had never made a political speech; never thought of such a thing; and had but four hours to put my ideas together; so, naturally, I hesitated about accepting the invitation. But, of a sudden, an inspiration came to me. I would make the speech, take Jeff Davis along to hear it, and so — convert him from the error of his ways, and make him a good citizen. Then, perhaps, he would vote the Republican ticket, and our good President would pardon him, and thus relieve me from longer acting as his keeper.

The hour for the meeting came, and Jeff went along willingly; but when he reached the doorway, firmly refused to go further than the hitching-post! Whether he knew he would have to listen to loyal sentiments, or objected to entering a building consecrated to the Unitarian faith, I could not conjecture; but there he stood, stubborn as a mule, and frowning as a reef of rocks at midnight.

I had heard that one Southerner could whip five Yankees, but that one Yankee could outgeneral a nation of Southerners; and I had some faith in the adage; but, could *I* outgeneral Jeff Davis? Admission was free; so the house was packed from basement to dome, with small boys perched in the windows; — and, as I went in, I said to the master of ceremonies: "Be good enough to keep the door open, or we shall suffocate."

I fired away right and left for an hour, and no doubt hit somebody; for the people, every now and then, went into tremendous spasms of hooting and shouting. But I cared little for them, — I kept my eye on the open door, and there Jeff stood listening, — quiet as a church mouse, and sober as a deacon! So, after all, I did outgeneral him.

On the way home the great Rebel was surly and silent as usual; but the next day seemed more

8*   L

subdued and thoughtful; and, within a week, actually extended his hand cordially to me, when one morning I went into his apartments. I had made an impression! The hardened sinner was being hopefully converted! True, he said nothing of voting the Republican ticket; but what of that? Mr. Lincoln was altogether too magnanimous to make that a condition of pardon; and yet — he might require some assurance of such amendment in Jeff's life and conversation as would make him a peaceful citizen.

To be able to give that, I thereafter bestowed upon him somewhat more of my personal attention; and — so the winter wore away, and the spring came, and the grass grew green in the meadows.

Jeff's moral progress during this time, owing to a nature singularly perverse and self-willed, was not rapid; but day by day we witnessed some improvement. He became less abrupt and surly in his general demeanor, and less violent in the company of strangers; but he never, after the date of my speech, alluded to political subjects, and therefore could not be counted among my proselytes; but I had the vanity to think that his moral regeneration began with my evening harangue. My twelve-year-old boy, however, ridiculed this notion; and with a modesty which, perhaps, he has inherited, insisted that Jeff's progress was due altogether to his own constant attention and kindness; adding, in that connection, with a grand flourish not altogether original, " Kindness, Dad! why, it 's the mightiest power in the universe! It will do for men, and is good for horses! It will melt steel, dissolve granite ; and, in the language of the poet, ' Soothe a savage, rend a rock, and split a cabbage !'"

" Our farm of three acres " is almost entirely grass and apple-trees ; and under these apple-trees, in pleasant weather, I am accustomed to lie and read, and muse, and write little stories for young people. Mr. Lincoln was then dead, so there was no hope of Jeff's pardon ; but, lying there one afternoon in June, I said to his affectionate friend, — my little boy, — " Would not Jeff enjoy this delicious shade, this pure air, this fragrant grass, and this pleasant prospect of the graveyard ?"

" O yes, father !" he shouted, springing to his feet and clapping his hands together. " Let him out !"

There is only a sunken wall about our premises, and the gates are slimsy affairs ; but Jeff we thought too much of a gentleman to attempt breaking from the enclosure. He is one of the Chivalry, — has a pedigree longer than my arm, — and, out of regard for his own reputation, and the fair fame of his famous ancestors, he would scorn to abuse my confidence by running away. This I thought; and, with a sweeping gesture, I said, " Let him out ! "

Out he came, greeted with the shouts of all the children; for, though not yet converted to the Republican faith, he was already a favorite with the whole family. First, he shook hands with all round, and then, taking " Billy Boy " on his back, raced about the " farm," trampling on the flower-beds, butting against the clothes-lines, overturning the rabbit-pens, and raising high havoc generally. He was taking a small " greenback " out of my treasury; but I gazed complacently on the demolition of my property; for were not the children enjoying themselves?

In the midst of this carnival, " Grandma " came racing from the house, — both pairs of spectacles on her nose, — and, going straight up to Jeff, said, in a tone in which anger and grief struggled for ascendency, " Ar' n't you ashamed of yourself? You are behaving like a young colt! If you go on at this rate, you 'll leave nothing standing on the premises." Jeff eyed her sorrowfully for a moment, then bowed his head, held out his hand, and, without a word, turned away, and all the rest of the day behaved like a gentleman.

After that we let him out whenever the weather was pleasant, and, for an individual of his peculiar disposition and habits, Jeff became wonderfully social and familiar. He would lie for hours under the apple-trees, poring over my books, while I sat beside him, reading or writing; or he would frolic with the boys, rolling over with them on the grass, letting them climb upon his back, hang about his neck, or get between his legs, just as if he were only a boy like themselves. But, strange as it may seem, his warmest affection was reserved for our Irish cook. That lady took complete possession of his heart, — though his stomach may have sympathized in the matter, for she pampered that organ outrageously. Every day, and at all hours of the day, he came to the kitchen window; and while he fed her affection with smiles and caresses, she fed his with apples, pears, peaches, dumplings, cream-cakes, and all manner of luxuries, until our provision bill grew to a size perfectly enormous. Affection is a good thing in its way, but this was carrying a good thing a little too far. It might lead to matrimony, and so deprive us of a valuable servant; or, what was of more consequence, it might swell our provision bill beyond my power to pay, and so bankrupt that worthy man, our grocer. Either way, a stop must be put to the intimacy.

One day we had tomato soup at dinner. When the dish was removed from the table, some one stole slyly into the kitchen, and gave it a strong dose of red pepper. As we expected, directly after dinner. Monsieur Jeff came to the window, and Madam Cook handed him the soup tureen. He took a deep draught of the savory fluid ; then, on a sudden, opened his mouth, tossed his nose up in the air, uttered some strange cries, and rolled over on the ground in frantic agony ; but he never again paid his addresses to the cook at the kitchen window.

With this enlargement of his liberty he developed a most voracious appetite. One day he broke into the garden, and consumed at one meal two hills of corn, six heads of cabbage, and at least a peck of tomatoes ; and I was deliberating whether considerations of economy would not force me to again reduce him to prison fare, when an event occurred which changed the current of his life, and brought him to an ignominious end.

As I have said, I let him out of prison, trusting to his honor — the honor of a Southern gentleman, with a long pedigree — that he would not attempt to escape, but would religiously keep within " the limits." But one day, not long ago, " Billy Boy " came rushing into the house with the tidings that " Deff Davis " was gone.

True enough, he had leaped the garden fence, and departed to parts unknown. After a long search, I found him in a very disreputable quarter of the town, and, with a heart heavy with wounded affection, escorted him back to his lodgings. And then that horse was tied to a beam in his stall, and his neck was encircled with a halter! He deserved his fate on his own account; and not only on his own account, but on account of bearing the name of the man who will go down as the most pernicious character in history.

CASTLE THUNDER.

I WAS in Richmond in the month of July, 1864, and, in company with the Rebel Exchange Commissioner, made a visit to Castle Thunder. It is a very famous prison; and, as you may not have seen it described, I have thought a short account of it might be interesting to you.

It is on the same street with the Libby Prison, and very near to it; but is much smaller than that building, and was used for the confinement of Northern civilians and Southern non-combatants, who had incurred the ill-will of the Rebel government. It has an odd name, and came by it in a singular manner. Before the war, it was the private residence of a well-to-do Irish gentleman, who had the misfortune to have a Xanthippe for a wife. The lady frequently performed on her husband's cranium with a broomstick, and this gave her the name, among the neighbors, of Mistress Thunder; and, by a natural transition, when her dwelling was transformed into a prison, it took the title of Castle Thunder.

As you may suppose, from its having once been a dwelling, this prison was more comfortable than the Libby, which had been used as a warehouse for the storage of ship-chandlery and tobacco. Its walls were plastered; but its rooms were small, and, when I visited them, filthy and desolate in the extreme. In each one a dozen haggard, homesick men were crowded; and there, in a space not more than twenty feet square, were obliged to eat, and sleep, and dream their lives away, day after day, and month after month, until the slow year rolled round, and went down to the other years which had gone to the great eternity.

I was not allowed to talk with any of the inmates, and so learned little of their real condition; but, since I have come away, a friend has given me an interesting account, written by Judge Finn, who was imprisoned in the Castle for many months. I will extract such portions of it as will give you an idea of the prison, and of the wretched life led there by the prisoners.

Mr. Finn was at one time Judge of the Superior Court in the city of New York, but before the war broke out removed to West Virginia, where he became State's Attorney. He was a thoroughly loyal man; and his strenuous opposition to the Rebellion having excited the hatred of the Rebel leaders, he was one night, early in 1864, kidnapped by a gang of ruffians, who bound him hand and foot, and conveyed him a prisoner to Richmond.

On arriving at the Rebel capital he was taken before a commissioner named Baxter, who, after administering to him an oath to make true answers to such questions as should be put to him, proceeded to examine and re-examine him, with a view to convicting him, on his own testimony, of treason against the Confederacy! After this examination he was taken to Castle Thunder, and — robbed of everything but the clothes he had on — was thrust into a filthy room, already occupied by half a score of half-starved men, ragged, and broken-spirited from long confinement.

The only furniture of this apartment was a splint broom, and a few shoddy blankets, alive with vermin. One of these blankets was furnished to each of the prisoners, and it was made to serve for both seat and bed; the prisoner, during the day, sitting on it in the Turkish fashion, and at night wrapping it about him, and lying down on the floor, with a billet of wood for a pillow. The room was infested with rats, bed-bugs, and "gray-backs," — creatures which, at the South, grow to an enormous size, and are "more terrible than an army with banners."

They overran everything. An hour every morning was spent by all of the prisoners in searching their garments, and exterminating these detestable vermin; but often, when they supposed they had cast out the last intruder, the Rebel soldiers on the floor above would have a "hoe-down," and a copious shower would again come upon the heads of the hapless victims. A gray-haired man of seventy, his sight dimmed with age, spent hours every day in removing these creatures from his clothing; and a sick prisoner was almost devoured by them. He became very weak, and was removed to the hospital, and, on changing his clothing, a couple of negro servants with a stout broom brushed more than a pint of "gray-backs" from his person.

The food given the prisoners was of the poorest and most unwholesome description. From the time of the Judge's arrival until the latter part of May, they received only two meals daily. At eight o'clock in the morning a breakfast, consisting of only eight ounces of stale corn-bread, and a cup of cold water, was served up to them; and at two o'clock in the afternoon they were given for dinner another eight ounces of corn-bread, and a pint of swill; and this was all they received until they were furnished with the same kind of breakfast on the following day.

This swill was made by putting a quart of cow-peas (a wild pea used at the South exclusively for feeding swine) into twelve quarts of water, and boiling it for an hour. Then it was served out in a pail so filthy as to be unfit for anything but a second-class pig-sty.

In the latter part of May the rations, though not increased in quantity, were somewhat improved in quality, — the prisoners receiving four ounces of cornbread, one ounce of meal, and half a gill of rice twice a day, at the same hours as before. But the bread, a portion of the time, was made of cow-feed, — corn and cobs ground up together, — and the meat, too, was often spoiled. The Judge has seen the cooks, in preparing fifty pounds of it for boiling, scrape off and take away eight quarts of maggots!

As may be readily conceived, life on such fare was only an apprenticeship to starvation. Every rat about the premises that could be caught was eaten. The Judge was told of this, and at first could not believe it; but one evening when he had wrapped himself in his blanket, and laid down to a troubled sleep, a prisoner in the adjoining apartment called to him for a little salt to season a fine rat he was roasting. The Judge hastened to the bars with the salt, and, sure enough, the man was cooking a large specimen over the jet of burning gas which illumined the dark apartment. When cooked, he salted and ate it, congratulating himself on being so fortunate as to have a "meat supper"! After that time the Judge saw hundreds of rats eagerly devoured by the starving inmates of the prison.

On another occasion a wealthy Pennsylvania farmer, who was captured by Stuart's raiders in the summer of 1862, and had been confined in the prison nearly two years, was seen to scrape the sawdust from one of the spittoons, mix it with water, and eat it with a spoon. When subsequently asked by his fellow-prisoners why he had done this, he answered : " I was so crazed with hunger that I did not know what I was doing."

The prisoners were allowed to send outside for any food, excepting vegetables ; but the most of them had no money to buy with, and were forced to die slowly on the prison rations. The Judge eked out his wretched fare with funds furnished him by a noble-hearted Virginian, — Mr. John Marselas, of Fauquier County. Why the prisoners were restricted from buying vegetables cannot be guessed, unless it was to bring upon them the awful scourge of scurvy, which is induced by an exclusive grain and meat diet. One of them, fearing an attack of

this disease, contrived to smuggle some potatoes into
his apartment; but the keeper found it out, and punished him by eight days' confinement underground,
in a dark and filthy cell, scarcely nine feet square,
and filled with an atmosphere so foul and oppressive
that it was next to impossible to breathe in it.

About a hundred prisoners were then confined in
the Castle; and, however well and strong they were
when they went there, they had nearly all fallen ill,
and wasted away on the wretched fare, till they were
the merest skeletons. Among them were boys of
tender years, and old men of eighty, who, suffering
with hunger, nearly naked, and almost devoured by
vermin, languished and died there, with no friend,
no wife, no child, no mother, to smooth their dying
pillows, or give them the consolations which, in the
hour of death, so lighten the painful passage to the
final home.

One of the prisoners was a lad of only fourteen,
the son of Captain John Snyder of Pendleton County,
West Virginia. He was captured at his home by
Imboden's horse-thieves, who, having a grudge against
his father, sent him as a prisoner to Richmond.

Another was Judge John McGuire, of the Carter
County Court, Kentucky. He had been arrested and
imprisoned two years before; but, after a month's

confinement, had taken the oath of allegiance to the Confederacy and been released. He at once tendered his services to his country, and was commissioned a Captain in an Ohio regiment. In the spring of 1864 he was again captured by the Rebels, conveyed to Richmond, and confined in the dungeon of Castle Thunder. It is supposed that he was afterwards hanged.

Another was Carter Newcomb, of Albemarle County, Virginia. He was a soldier of 1812; and, being suspected of loving the old flag, was visited by the Rebel provost-guard, who, representing themselves as deserters from the Confederate army, asked him his opinion of the war. He was working in the field; and laying down his axe, and resting on a fence he was building, he told them that, though he was over threescore years and ten, he was obliged to till his land alone, and earn a livelihood for his family, because his sons, who had assisted him, had all been conscripted by the Rebels, and he added: "If the men who brought on this war had to fight it out themselves, I would not care." For these words he was arrested and incarcerated in Castle Thunder !

One of the most aged and venerable of the prisoners was Thomas Tiff, an eminent lawyer of Jackson, Mississippi. He owned a plantation of several thousand acres, on which he lived with a little grandson of only twelve years, who was the last of all his kindred. After his State seceded, he still expressed himself in favor of the Union; and, at last, a band of Rebels came and laid waste his plantation, robbing him of all he had, — thrusting their hands into his pockets to steal his money, and even into his mouth for the gold plate attached to the set of false teeth he wore. Then they took him and his little grandson to Richmond, and lodged them in Castle Thunder. There, in the winter, Mr. Tiff became coatless, and the Rebel officials offered him a new garment. He examined it, and finding it was such as was worn by the Rebel soldiers, refused to accept it, saying he would not disgrace himself by wearing the garb of the armed enemies of the nation. He spent the winter with only an old blanket about his shoulders; and he died, — died in prison, a martyr to freedom and his country. There are men at the North who, even now, grumble about the war, and groan over their taxes; but this noble Mississippian freely gave his all, even his life, as a sacrifice for liberty.

There were several ladies in the prison; and among them Miss Mary E. Walker, Assistant Surgeon of the Fifty-second Regiment of Ohio Infantry. She was one day taking a morning ride in Georgia, and, losing her way, rode into the Rebel lines and was captured. She was afterwards exchanged, and returned to her regiment.

The Judge passed several weary months in the prison; but at last was exchanged, and returned to his home in safety. As soon as he was captured, the Governor of West Virginia arrested several wealthy Secessionists of the Shenandoah Valley, and held them as hostages for his return. He also did all in his power to effect his release; and, early in May, paroled one of the hostages, and sent him to Richmond to accomplish it. The Rebel Secretary of War made out an order for Judge Finn's liberation, and forwarded a copy by the hostage to the Governor of West Virginia, but he kept the Judge in prison. The Governor, however, was not to be thus duped by the Rebel Secretary. He refused to release the hostages until Judge Finn was safely returned to his home.

On the 25th of May, another hostage was paroled and sent to Richmond, to learn why the Judge had not been released. He saw the Rebel officials, and they assured him that he was released early in the month, and would go North by the first

9   M

flag of truce boat, but had been detained because no boat had since then departed from Richmond. This was entirely false, yet they had the perfidy to put it in writing, sign it, and then ask Judge Finn to give it his signature. He refused, telling them plainly that they knew well he had not been released, and that two boats had left Richmond since the date they had mentioned. Thus they failed in their base design; but the Judge remained a prisoner.

Finally, on the 29th of June, Hon. G. H. C. Rowe of Fredericksburg, Va., came to him and asked his influence to effect the exchange of some Fredericksburg citizens, who were held as hostages for some wounded soldiers alleged to have been betrayed into the hands of the Confederates by Mayor Slaughter. The Judge saw that the Rebels were aiming to drive a good bargain, — to exchange him for a Fredericksburg citizen, and for the two hostages besides; but confinement had worn upon him, he was failing fast, and it was plain he could not endure prison-life more than a few weeks longer; so he consented to the arrangement, and was let out of prison.

On the next day he was sent to the Libby by order of the Provost-Marshal, who directed the keeper, Major Turner to send him North by flag of truce on

the following morning. The hour for the departure
of the flag at last arrived, and with joyful emotions
the Judge fell into the ranks with about fifty soldiers
and four other Union citizens; and, marching down
the main street to the railway station, was soon
aboard of the cars, and on his way to Hanover Junction. Arrived there, the prisoners were told they
must walk all the way to Occoquan, — a distance of
sixty miles. They could not have done it had they
been journeying towards Richmond; but the prospect of home and freedom buoyed them up, and they
felt equal to anything.

They marched under guard of a dozen Richmond
cavalry, who were mounted on splendid horses. They
were obliged. to wade the North Anna River, where
the water was two and a half feet in depth; and the
guards grumbled because they took time to remove
their boots and roll up their trousers! By noon
the Judge had become so much fatigued that he
could not keep up with the remainder of the column,
and, regardless of the threats of the Rebel Lieutenant in command, fell behind with two of the guards,
who, unlike their comrades, had some feeling of humanity. He marched until two o'clock of the next
morning before he reached the place where the others had encamped for the night. The Lieutenant

awoke about four o'clock, and observing the Judge, ordered a guard to take him, and ten others who had also lagged behind, and march forward with them immediately, while the rest of the party remained and had breakfast. He said this would teach them to keep up another time.

When they had arrived within three miles of Fredericksburg, several of the prisoners had become so completely worn out that they could proceed no further. They were then allowed to hire a horse-cart of a lady of Southern principles, who, for nine dollars in greenbacks, consented to send them on to the village. She desired, she said, to get some goods through the blockade, or she would not have consented to forward them for any amount of money. As it was, she would let no one ride in the cart but residents of the sacred soil of Virginia.

At Fredericksburg the weary party remained over night, and Union citizens visited their camp, giving them warm food, hot coffee, and linen to bandage their swollen limbs. There the guards left for Richmond, after admonishing them to work for peace, and vote for General McClellan.

With a new guard and a white flag they set out again the next morning, and reached Occoquan — a town on the Occoquan River — after a toilsome march of two days. In the river lay the flag of truce boat; they entered it with joyful hearts, and were soon on their way to Alexandria. As the boat glided into the rippling Potomac, the flag of truce was lowered, and the starry banner flung to the breeze, amid the wild huzzas of the returned prisoners.

The Judge arrived at Alexandria attired in a Rebel coat and hat, and a pair of stockings which scarcely could hold together. The hat he had borrowed, (the Rebels having stolen his,) and the coat he had obtained in an exchange which realized for him fifteen dollars of Confederate money, that he invested in breadstuffs. As he marched from the wharf to the Provost-Marshal's office in Alexandria, an old lady pointed at him, and, deeming him a suspicious character, exclaimed: "See there! they have caught one bushwacker, thank the Lord!"

The Provost-Marshal was very kind to the prisoners, and procured a conveyance for those who could not walk, in which the Judge took passage, with some of the returned soldiers, for Camp Distribution, about two miles south of Washington. This camp covered many acres, and was embowered in splendid forest-trees; and its wide streets, pebbled walks, and neatly arranged barracks gave it the appearance of a thriving town.

Here the Judge remained one day, and then Uncle Sam gave him a pass over the railway, and he set out for his home in West Virginia.

But his troubles were not yet over. He had been at home only two days, when a party of Rebels rode up to his house, and demanded to see the State's Attorney, who had just graduated from Richmond. Luckily, he had warning of their approach, and was absent. After that he had a varied experience; but he was never again within the walls of Castle Thunder.

THE GREAT PRISON.

SINCE I wrote the last story I have been again in prison. Many people consider it a great disgrace to get into prison, and think that all prisons are very bad places ; but it is not so. Some of the best men who ever lived have passed years in dungeons ; and the prison I have been in is a very comfortable place, — a great deal more comfortable than the houses which one half of its inmates have been accustomed to live in. So one cold morning, not a great while ago, with my eyes wide open, and knowing very well what I was about, I walked into it.

All of you have heard of this famous prison, for it is talked about all over the world ; so I have thought you might like to know how it looks, and something about the people who were in it, and the important events which transpired in connection with it during the great Rebellion.

It is called Camp Douglas, and is located on the shore of Lake Michigan, about three miles from the

city of Chicago, and is very large, — a good deal
larger than a small farm, — and had more inhabitants than any two of the biggest villages in the
country.   It is enclosed by a close board fence, and
covered with just such a roof as Boston Common.
The fence is so high that you cannot see the whole
of the prison at once, unless you go up in a balloon,
or climb to the top of the tall observatory which
some enterprising Yankee has built on the street
opposite the front gateway.   But it would cost
nearly as much as you paid for this book to enter
that observatory, and you might break your necks
if you should go up in a balloon; so here is a
bird's-eye view of the whole prison, and, if you
choose, you may see it all for nothing, while seated
in your own cosey homes, with your heads on your
shoulders, and your heels on the fire-fender.

If you look at the lower left-hand corner of this
picture you will see an engine and a train of cars,
and below them a vacant spot resembling water.
That water is a few buckets-full of the great lake on
whose shore Chicago stands.   Rising up from it in
a gentle slope are fenced fields and pleasant gar-
dens, dotted here and there with trees and houses,
and beyond them — a mere white line in the picture — is the public road which runs in front of the

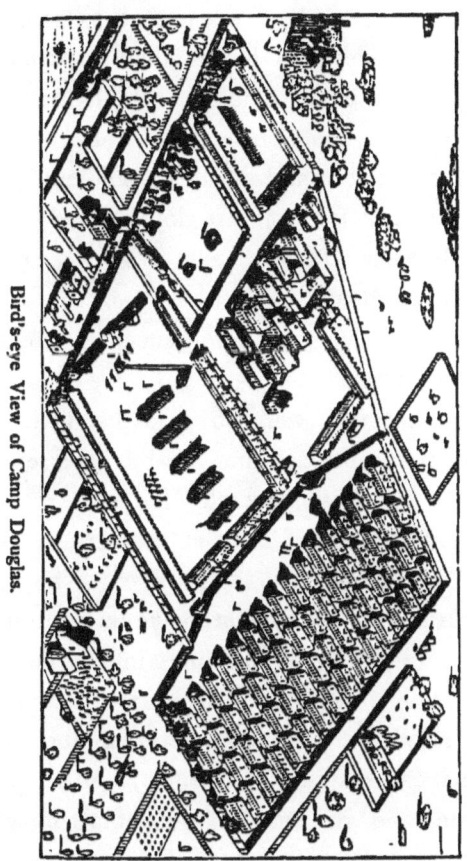

Bird's-eye View of Camp Douglas.

Camp.   Midway along this road, and right where
the row of trees begins, is the principal gateway of
the prison.   It looks like the entrance to some old
castle, being broader and higher than a barn-door,
and having half a dozen soldiers, with loaded muskets and fixed bayonets, pacing to and fro before
it.   If you are not afraid of these soldiers, — and
you need not be, for you are loyal young folks,
and they all wear Uncle Sam's livery, — we will
speak to one of them.

"There is pos-i-tive-ly no admittance, sir," he says,
turning to walk away.

We know that very well, so I take a little note
from my pocket, and ask him to be good enough
to send it to the Commandant.   He eyes the note
for a moment, and then looks at us, very much as
if we owed him a quarter's rent.   You see he needs
to be vigilant, for we might have a contraband
mail, or a dozen infernal machines in our pockets;
but, touching his cap, he disappears through the
gateway.   However, he soon returns, and, again
touching his cap, says: "Gentlemen," — (he means
you and me, and he has forgotten that some of
you are young ladies,) — "the Colonel will be happy to see you."

We follow him through the gate-house, where a

score of soldiers are lounging about, and into a
broad, open yard, paved with loose sand ; and then
enter a two-story wooden building, flanked by long
rows of low-roofed cabins, and overshadowed by a
tall flag-staff. In the first room that we enter, half
a dozen officers are writing at as many desks ; and
in the next, a tall, fine-looking man in a colonel's
uniform is pacing the floor, and rapidly dictating to
a secretary who sits in the corner. He stops when
he perceives us, and extends his hand in so friendly
and cordial a way that we take a liking to him at
once. But when he asks us to sit down, and begins
to talk, we take a stronger liking to him than before, and wonder if this quiet, unassuming gentleman, with this pleasant smile, and open, frank,
kindly face, can be the famous Colonel Sweet, whose
wonderful sagacity ferreted out the deepest-laid conspiracy that ever was planned, and whose sleepless
vigilance saved Chicago and one half of the West
from being wrapped in flames.

Not wanting to encroach too long on his valuable
time, we briefly explain our business, and, seating
himself at his table, he writes, in a straight up and
down hand — for his fingers are stiffened by a wound
in his arm — the following pass : " Permit —— ——
to enter and leave the camp, and to inspect the

prison, and converse with the prisoners, at his pleasure."

With this pass in our hand we are about to leave the room, when the Colonel taps a bell, and an officer enters, whom he introduces to us, and directs him to escort us about the camp. Thus doubly provided, we emerge from head-quarters, and enter a large enclosure where more than a thousand men are under review. The old flag is flying from a tall staff at one end of this enclosure, and at the other end, and on both of its sides, are long rows of soldiers' barracks.

However, we have seen reviews and barracks before, so we do not linger here, but follow our escort, Lieutenant Briggs, into the adjoining yard.

Here are the hospitals, those two-story wooden buildings, nicely battened and whitewashed, which you see in the picture. In each story of these buildings is a long, high-studded apartment, with plastered walls, clean floors, and broad, cheerful windows, through which floods of pure air and sunshine pour in upon the dejected, homesick prisoners. These rooms are the homes of the sick men, and here they linger all through the long days, and the still longer nights, tied down to narrow cots by cords stronger than were ever woven by man. About five hundred are always here, and four or five of them are borne out daily to the little burial-ground just outside the prison walls.* This may appear sad; but if you reflect that there are constantly from eight to nine thousand prisoners in the camp, four or five will seem a very small number to die every day among so many idle, homesick, broken-spirited men. More people die of idleness, low spirits, and homesick-

* On November 19th, 1864, there were 8,308 prisoners in Camp Douglas, 513 invalids in the hospital, and 4 deaths among the whole. On November 20th, there were 8,295 prisoners, 508 in hospital, and 5 deaths. On November 21st, 8,290 prisoners, 516 in hospital, and 4 deaths. Compare this mortality with that of our own men in the Confederate prisons! When only six thousand were at Belle Isle, *eighty-five* died every day; and when nine thousand — about the average number confined at Camp Douglas — were at Salisbury, Mr. Richardson reports that *one hundred and thirty* were daily thrown into a rude cart, and dumped, like decayed offal, into a huge hole outside the camp. The mortality at Andersonville and the other Rebel prisons was as great as this, and even greater; but I have not the reports at hand, and cannot; therefore, give the statistics accurately. If our men were not deliberately starved and murdered, would such excessive mortality have existed in the Rebel prisons?

All of the prisoners at Camp Douglas were well fed, well clothed, and well cared for in every way. Some Northern traitors have said they were not, but *they were.* I was among them for three days, mixed freely with them, and lived on their

ness than of all the diseases and all the doctors in the world; so, my young folks, keep busy, keep cheerful, and never give way to homesickness if you can help it, and then you possibly may outlive Old Parr himself; and he, some folks say, never would have died at all, if he had not, in his old age, foolishly taken to tobacco and bad whiskey.

After passing an hour in the hospitals, we go into

rations, and I know whereof I affirm. No better food than theirs was ever tasted, and, with the best intentions, I could not, for the life of me, eat more than three fourths of the quantity that was served out to the meanest prisoner. As I have said, there were, on the 19th of November, 1864, 513 prisoners in the hospital. On that day there were issued to them (I copy from the official requisition, which is before me) 395 pounds of beef, 60 pounds of pork, 525 pounds of bread, 25 pounds of beans, 25 rations of rice, 14 pounds of coffee, 35 pounds of sugar, 250 rations of vinegar, 250 rations of soap, and 250 rations of salt. This was the daily allowance while I was there. In addition, there had been issued to this hospital, within the previous fifteen days, 250 pounds of butter, 66 pounds of soda crackers, 30 bushels of potatoes, 10 bushels of onions, 20 bushels of turnips, 10 bushels of dried apples, 3 dozen of squashes, 2 dozen of chickens, 250 dozen of eggs, and 25 dozen of cabbages. Let any well man divide this quantity of provender by 500, and then see how long it will take him to eat it. If he succeeds in disposing of it in one day, let me advise him to keep the fact from his landlady, or the price of his board may rise.

the bakery, a detached building in the same enclosure. Here a dozen prisoners, bred to the "profession," are baking bread, and preparing other food for the invalids. The baking is done in immense ovens, and the dough is kneaded in troughs which are two feet wide, three feet deep, and forty feet long! From this building, where food is prepared to support life, we go into another, where nostrums are mixed that destroy it. Here are drugs enough to kill every man in the camp. They are dispensed by a Confederate surgeon, who was an apothecary at home. He complains that his business is alarmingly dull, and, from the way it is falling off, fears that the world is growing wiser, — so wise that, when the war is over, his occupation may be gone. It seems a sad prospect to him, but we console ourselves with the thought that what may be his loss will be other people's gain.

From the drug store we pass to the rear of the open yard which you see in the picture, and pause before the little low building on the right. This is the quarters of Captain Wells Sponable, the inspector of the prison ; and over against it is a gateway, which opens into the large enclosure where the prisoners are confined. Lieutenant Briggs raps at the door of this little building, and in a moment a tall, compactly-built man, with broad, open features, and hair enough on his face to stuff a moderate-sized mattress, make his appearance. He glances at the pass which we present to him, and then says, in a rapid way, jerking out his words as if his jaws were moved by a crank, — "I'm glad to see you. Come in. I'll go with you myself."

We go into his quarters, and after half an hour's pleasant conversation, — in which we find out that the Captain, though blunt and outspoken, is one of the most agreeable, whole-souled men in the world, — we follow him and the Lieutenant into the prison-

yard. Here is the Captain's picture, and I want you to take a good look at it, for I am sure you will like him when I have told you more about him.

The prison-yard is an enclosure of about twenty acres, surrounded by a board fence fourteen feet high, and guarded by thirty sentinels, who are posted on a raised platform just outside the fence, and pace the rounds at all hours of the day and night. Their beats are only a hundred and twenty feet apart, and on dark nights the camp is

illuminated by immense reflecting-lamps, placed on the walls and at the ends of the streets, so that it is next to impossible for anything to occur within it, at any time, without the knowledge of the guards. Inside the enclosure, and thirty feet from the fence, is a low railing entirely surrounding the camp. This is the dead line. Whoso goes beyond this railing, at any hour of the day or night, is liable to be shot down without warning. In making our rounds the Captain occasionally stepped over it, but I never followed him without instinctively looking up to see if the sentry's musket was not pointed at me. Half a dozen poor fellows have been shot while crossing this rail on a desperate run for the fence and freedom.

A part of the prison yard, as you will see in the picture, is an open space ; — and there the men gather in squads, play at games, or hold "political meetings"; but the larger portion is divided into streets, and occupied by barracks. The streets are fifty feet wide, and extend nearly the whole length and breadth of the enclosure. They are rounded up in the middle, and have deep gutters at the sides, so that in wet weather the rain flows off, and leaves them almost as dry as a house floor. The barracks are one-story wooden buildings, ninety feet long and twenty-four feet wide, and stand on posts four feet from the ground. They are elevated in this manner to prevent the prisoners tunnelling their way out of camp, as some of Morgan's men did while Colonel DeLand had charge of the prison. Here is a view of one of the streets, taken from a drawing made by a young prisoner, who, though scarcely yet a man, has been confined at Camp Douglas eighteen long months. All of the engravings which follow in this and the next chapter are from drawings made by him; and when you look at the skill displayed in them, I know you will think, with me, that one who has such talent should not be forced to idle his life away in a prison.

Each barrack is divided into two rooms; — one a square apartment, where the prisoners do their cooking; the other a long hall, with three tiers of bunks on either side, where they do their sleeping. The larger rooms are furnished with benches and a stove, have several windows on each side, and ventilators on the roof, and are as comfortable places to stay in as one could expect in a prison. But the engraving opposite will give you a better idea of them than any description I could make.

The most perfect discipline prevails in the camp. Each day is distinctly "ordered," and no one is al-

lowed to depart from the rules. At sunrise the drum
beats the reveille, and every man turns out from his
bunk. In half an hour breakfast is ready, and in
another hour the roll is called. Then the eight thousand or more prisoners step out from their barracks,
and, forming in two lines in the middle of the street,
wait until the officer of the day calls their names.
Those who have the misfortune to be at the foot of
the column may have to wait half an hour before they
hear the welcome sound ; and in cold or rainy weather this delay is not over-agreeable. With a *feeling*
sense of its discomforts, our artist has represented
such a scene in the accompanying sketch.

After roll-call the "details" go about their work,
and the other men do as they like until twelve
o'clock, when they are all summoned to dinner. The
"details" are prisoners who have applied to take
the oath of allegiance, and who are consequently
trusted rather more than the others. They are em-
ployed in various ways, both inside and outside of
the prison, but not outside of the camp. They are
paid regularly for this work, and it affords them a
small fund, with which they buy tobacco and other
little luxuries that they have been accustomed to.
Those who are not so fortunate as to have work supply themselves with these "indispensables" by sell-

ing offal, old bones, surplus food, and broken bottles
to an old fellow who makes the rounds of the camp
every few days with a wagon or a wheelbarrow.
Here he is with his "Ammunition train."

After dinner the "details" go again to work, and
the loungers to play, though almost all of them find
some work if it is nothing more than whittling.   They
seem to have the true Anglo-Saxon horror of nothing to do, and therein show their relationship to us ;
for, say what we may, the great mass of Southerners
are merely transplanted Yankees, differing from the
original Jonathan only as they are warped by slavery,
or crushed by slave-holders.   That number of Eng-
lishmen, hived within the limits of twenty acres, would

take to grumbling, Germans to smoking, Irishmen to brawling, Frenchmen to swearing ; but these eight thousand· Southerners have taken to whittling, and that proves them Yankees, — and no amount of false education or political management can make them anything else. One has whittled a fiddle from a pine shingle ; another, a clarionet from an ox-bone ; a third, a meerschaum from a corn-cob ; a fourth, a water-wheel — which he says, will propel machinery without a waterfall — from half a dozen sticks of hickory ; a fifth, with no previous practice, makes gold rings from brass, and jet from gutta percha ; and, to crown ·all, a sixth has actually whittled a whistle — and a whistle that " blows " — out of a pig's tail !

But they showed the trading as well as the inventive genius of Yankees. One has swapped coats until he has got clear through his elbows ; another, pantaloons, until they scarcely come below his knees ; another, hats, until he has only part of a rim, and the " smallest showing " of a crown, — and yet every time, — so he says, — he has had the best of the trade ; and another regularly buys out the old apple-woman, and *peddles* her stock about the camp at the rate of a dollar " a grab," payable in greenbacks.

With such unmistakable manifestations of national character, no one can doubt that these people are

Yankees, and Yankees too, who, with free schools and free institutions, would be the "smartest" and "'cutest" people in the world.

At sunset the drums beat the "retreat," and all the prisoners gather to their quarters, from which they do not again emerge until the reveille is sounded in the morning. Then the candles are lighted, and each barrack presents a scene worthy of a painter. Look into any of them after nightfall, and you will see at least seventy motley-clad, rollicking, but good-natured "natives," engaged in all imaginable kinds of employment. Some are writing, some reading newspapers or musty romances, some playing at euchre, seven-up, or rouge-et-noir; but more are squatted on the floor, or leaning against the bunks, listening to the company "oracle," who, nursing his coat-tails before the stove, is relating "moving accidents by flood and field," fighting his battles over again, or knocking "the rotten Union inter everlastin' smash." One of the most notable of these "oracles" is "your feller-citizen, Jim Hurdle, sir."

Jim is a "character," and a "genius" of the first order. His coat is decidedly seedy, his hat much the worse for wear, and his trousers so out at the joints that he might be suspected of having spent his whole life on his knees; but he is a "born gentleman," above work, and too proud "to be be-

holden to a kentry he has fit agin." He knows a little
of everything under the sun, and has a tongue that
can outrun any steam-
engine in the universe.
The stories he tells never
were beaten. They are
" powerful " stories, —
so powerful that, if you
don't keep firm hold of
your chairs, they may
take you right off your
feet. Once, he says, he
shot eighteen hundred
squirrels in a day, with
a single-barrelled shot-
gun. At another time he

met a panther in a wood, and held him at bay for
nearly six hours by merely looking at him. Again,
when he was crossing a brook on horseback, the
bridge was carried away by a freshet, and floated
two miles down the stream, where it lodged in the
top of a tree. As nothing could be done, he dismounted, and went quietly to sleep on the bridge
until the morning. In the morning the "run" had
subsided, but the horse and the bridge were still
perched in the top of the tree. "I tried to coax
the critter to git down,"—so the tale runs, — "but

he would n't budge; and I piked for home, for I know'd oats 'ud bring him. And shore 'nuff they did. The hoss had n't more 'n smelled of the peck-measure I tuck to him, 'fore down he come, quicker 'n lightnin' ever shot from a thunder-cloud."

"But how did the horse get down?"

"How! Why, hind eend afore, like any other hoss; and, stranger, that ar hoss was 'bout the laziest critter ye ever know'd on. He was so lazy that I had to hire another hoss to holp him dror his last breath."

Jim's stories lack the very important element of truth, and in that respect are not unlike some other stories you may have read; but they do illustrate two prominent characteristics of all Southern people, — a propensity to brag, and a disposition to magnify everything.

Mr. Hurdle is guarded in expressing his political opinions, but one of his comrades assured me that he had lost all faith in the Confederacy. "The Confederacy, sir!" he is reported to have said, "ar busted, — gone all to smash. It ar rottener nur any egg that ever was sot on, and deader nur any door-nail that ever was driv."

"But it bites a little yit, Jim," said a comrade.

"Bites!" echoed Jim. "Of course it do. So will

a turkle arter his head ar cut off. I know'd one o' them critters onst that a old darky dercapertated. The next day he was 'musin' hisself pokin' sticks at him, and the turkle was biting at 'em like time. Then I says to the darky, 'Pomp, I thought he war dead.' — 'Well, he am massa,' says Pomp, 'but the critter don't know 'nuff to be sensible ob it.' So, ye see, the Confederacy ar dead, but Jeff Davis and them sort o' fellers don't know enough to be sensible of it."

But "Nine o'clock, and lights out!" sounds along the sentry-lines, and every candle is extinguished in a twinkling. The faintest glimmer after that hour will draw a leaden messenger that may snuff out some poor fellow's light forever. Not a year ago a Rebel sergeant, musing by the stove in the barrack we are in, heard that cry repeated. He looked up, and seeing nothing but darkness, went on musing again. The stove gave out a faint glow which shone through the window, and the sentinel, mistaking it for the light of a candle, fired, crushing the poor fellow's arm at the elbow. A few nights later another stove gave out a faint glow, and another sentry sent a leaden messenger through the window, mortally wounding — the stove-pipe. Both sentinels were punished, but that did not save the sergeant's arm, or mend the stove-pipe.

10

AMONG THE PRISONERS.

THE day is Sunday, and we spend it among the prisoners. It is general inspection day at the prison, and, by invitation of the Captain, we go early to witness the interesting turn-out. It is a real turn-out, for every prisoner in the camp on this day turns out from his quarters, and, with all his household goods about him, waits in the street opposite his barrack until every bed, and blanket, and jack-knife, and jews-harp, and fiddle, and trinket, and "wonderful invention" in the prison is examined and passed upon by the Inspector. Of the latter articles, as I have said, there is an infinite variety, but of necessary clothing there is nothing to spare. A mattress, a blanket or two, a hat, a coat, a pair of trousers and brogans, and an extra shirt, are the sum total of each one's furniture and wearing-apparel. Every man's person must be cleanly, and his clothing as tidy as circumstances will permit; and woe to the foolish "native" who has neglected to bathe, or forgotten to exterminate his little brood of domestic animals. A high-pressure scrubbing, or a march about camp in a packing-box, branded ".Vermin," is his inevitable doom. This three hours' review is an irksome ordeal to the prisoners, but blessed be the man who invented it; for it keeps the doctors idle, and gives an easy life to the grave-diggers.

It may be you have somewhere· read that "the proper study of mankind is man." If you have and believe it, you will he glad to go with me down the lines, and study these people; and if you do this, and keep your eyes open, you will learn something of the *real* Southern man; and you 'might waste years among the " Chivalry " and not do that. The "Chivalry" are not Southern *men*, they are only Southern *gentlemen*, and counterfeit gentlemen at that. But now we will go down the column.

The first man we meet is not a man. He is only a boy, — a slender, pale-faced boy, with thin, white hands, and wan, sad, emaciated features, on which "Exchanged" is written as legibly as anything that ever was printed. But he will not wait· the slow movements of the Exchange Commissioners. The grim old official who has him in charge is altogether too wise to wrangle about the terms of cartels, where the lives of men are in question.

He receives our advances in a shy, reserved way, and it takes many kind words to draw from him more than a monosyllable. But kind words are a power. They cost less, and buy more, than anything else in the world. I never knew one of them to be wasted; and not one is wasted now, for very soon they reach the boy's heart, and with moistened eye and quivering lip he tells us his story. It is a simple story, — only a little drama of humble life, with no fine ladies in rouge and satins and furbelows, and no fine gentlemen with waving plumes and gilded swords, and shining patent-leathers, dawdling about the stage, or making silly faces at the foot-lights. Its characters are only common people who *do* something, — *produce* something, — and so leave the world a little better for their living in it. But it is only a short story, just a little drama, and I will let it pass before you.

Now the curtain rises, and the play begins.

We see a little log cottage among the mountains, with a few cattle browsing in the woods, and a few acres of waving corn and cotton. Grape-vines and honeysuckles are clambering over the doorway, and roses and wild-flowers are growing before the windows, and — that is all. But it is a pleasant little cottage, all attractive without, and all cheerful within.

The candles are not lighted, but a great wood-fire is blazing on the hearth, sending a ·rich, warm glow through all the little room; and the family have gathered round it for the evening. The older brother is mending harness before the fire; the little sister is knitting beside him; the younger brother and another one — nearer and dearer to him than brother or sister — are seated on the low settle in the chimney-corner; and the aged mother is reading aloud from a large book which lies open on the centre-table. We can't see the title of this book, but its well-worn leaves show that it must be the family Bible. She closes it after a while, and, the older brother laying aside his work, they all kneel down on the floor together. Then the mother prays, — not a fashionable prayer, with big, swelling words, and stilted, high-flown sentences, such as you sometimes hear on a Sunday, — but a low, simple, earnest petition to Him who is her Father and her Friend, who knows her every want, and loves her as one of His dear children.

It is scarcely over when the door opens, and five ruffianly-looking men enter the room. Four of them wear the gray livery of the Rebels; the other is clad in a motley uniform, part gray, part reddish-brown, and the other part the tawny flesh-color which peeps through the holes in his trousers. He looks for all the world like the tall fellow yonder, — farther down the lines, — the one in ragged "butternuts" and tattered shirt, with that mop of bushy black hair, and that hang-dog, out-at-the-elbow look. They both are conscript officers, and the one in the play has come to arrest the two young men, who have refused to obey the conscription.

The older brother rises to his feet, and, with a look of honest scorn and defiance, says: "I will not go with you. No power on earth shall make me fight against my country." No more is spoken, but two of the soldiers seize the younger brother, and two others advance upon the older one, while the officer — standing by at a safe distance — gets the handcuffs ready. In less time than it takes to tell it, the two other men have measured their length on the floor; but the officer springs backward, and draws his revolver. He is about to fire, when the older brother catches the weapon, and attempts to wrest it from his hand. They grapple for an instant, and the pistol goes off in the struggle. A low scream follows, — but the officer falls to the floor, and the older brother bounds away into the darkness.

In a moment every one is on his feet again; but not a step is taken, not a movement made. Even

these hardened men stand spell-bound and horror-
stricken by the scene that is before them. There,
upon the floor, the blood streaming from a ghastly
wound in her neck, lies the fair young girl who was
the sunshine of that humble home. The younger
brother is holding her head in his lap, and moaning
as if his heart were breaking, and the aged mother
is kneeling by her side, trying to stanch the streaming blood; but the crimson river is running fast, and
with it a sweet young life is flowing, — flowing on
to the great sea, where the sun shines and the sweet
south-wind blows forever.

The soldiers look on in silence; but the officer
speaks at last. "Come," he says; "it 's all over
with the gal. The boy must go with me."

"He shall not go," says the mother. "Leave us
alone to-night. You can murder him in the morning!"

The look and tone of that woman would move a
mountain. They move even these men, for they turn
away, and then the scene changes.

Now we see a great wood, — one of those immense pine-forests which cover nearly all of Upper
Georgia. The baying of hounds is heard in the
distance, and upon the scene totters a weak, fam-
ished man, with bleeding feet and matted hair, and

torn, bedraggled clothing. He sinks down at the foot of a tree, and draws a revolver. He knows the hounds are close at hand ; and, starving, hunted down as he is, he clings to life with all the energy of the young blood that is in him. Soon he staggers to his feet, and puts up his weapon. He says nothing, but the look in his eye tells of some desperate resolve he has taken. He tries to climb the tree, but the branches are high up in the air; his strength fails, and he falls backward. Again he tries, and this time is successful. A moment more and he would have been too late, for the hounds have tracked him far, and now, with wild howls, are right upon him. Down among those furious beasts he would be torn limb from limb in an instant, — and O horror! the branch bends, — his arm trembles, — he is losing his hold, — he is falling! No! he catches by a stouter limb, and once more is in safety. Meanwhile, the hounds are howling hungrily below, and the shouts of men are heard, far away at the westward. He listens, and, drawing himself nearer the trunk of the tree, takes out the revolver. Five charges are left, and every cap is perfect. His life is lost; but for how many lives can he · sell it?

The shouts grow louder, and, guided by the cry

of the dogs, the men come rushing through the forest.
One nears the tree — hears a shot — staggers back —
and falls headlong. Another comes on, and another,
and still another, and they all give up man-hunting
forever! The rest pause, and hide behind trees,
warned by the fate of their comrades. Four lives
for one! Shall he have another, or shall his last
bullet be wasted? At last a man springs into sight,
and gains a nearer cover. The pistol cracks, — a
rifle-shot cuts the air, and —— It is a dizzy height,
— our heads swim, and we turn away, while the
scene changes.

Once more we see the little log cottage among
the mountains. It is night, and midwinter. The
snow lies deep in the woods, and the wind sighs
mournfully around the little cabin, and has a melan-
choly shiver in its voice, as it tries to whistle "Old
Hundred" through the key-hole. The same wood-
fire is burning low on the hearth, and the same aged
mother and little sister are seated before it. The
same, and not the same, — for the roses are gone
from the young girl's cheeks, and the mother is wasted
to a shadow! The cattle are stolen from the fields,
and the last kernel of corn has been eaten. What
will keep them from starving? The mother opens
the Book, and reads how Elijah was fed by the ravens.

10* o

Will not the same Lord feed them? She will trust Him!

And again the scene changes. It is the same play, but only one of the players is living. He is the pale-faced boy in the prison. Kindly and gently we say to him: "You look sick; should you not be in the hospital?"

"I think not, — I like the sun," he answers. "When the colder weather comes, I may have to go there."

He *will* go, and — then the curtain will fall, and the little play be over!

Is it not a thrilling drama? With slight variations of scenery, it has been acted in ten thousand Southern homes, with Satan for manager and Jefferson Davis for leading actor and "heavy villain."

As we go down the lines, we pass the conscript officer I have alluded to. We do not speak with him, for a look at the outside of "the house he lives in" represses all desire to become acquainted with the inside. Virtue and nobleness can no more dwell in such a body as his, than the Christian virtues can flourish in a hyena. The thing is an impossibility, and the man is not to blame for it. His very name is suggestive of what he may come to. Alter one letter of it, and it would be J. B. Hemp, —

which, you all know, is the abreviation for Jerked
By Hemp; and that is the usual end of such people.

As we pass this man, the Captain — who is making the rounds with us, while the Lieutenant goes
on with the inspection — tells us something about
him. He is despised by every one in the camp;
and though the Captain makes it a principle to show
no ill-will or partiality to any of the prisoners, he
has to feel the general dislike to him. He is prob-
ably about as mean as
a man ever gets to be.
A short time ago he
planned an escape by
the "Air Line"; and,
with the help of another
prisoner, made a ladder,
and hid it away under
the floor of his barrack.
The Captain found it
out, and charged him
with it. He denied it

stoutly, but the Captain told him to bring out the
ladder. With great reluctance, he finally produced
it; and, placing it against the side of the barrack,
the Captain said: "My man, this is a good ladder,
— a very good ladder; and it ought to be used.

Now, suppose you let it stand where it is, and walk up and down upon it for a week. The exercise will do you good, and the ladder, you know, was made expressly for you." The prisoner was immensely pleased at the idea of so light a punishment, (attempts to escape, you know, are punished severely in all prisons,) and began the walk, laughing heartily at the "fool of a Yankee," who thought that sort of exercise any hardship to a man accustomed to using his legs.

Crowds gathered round to see him, and for a time everything went right merrily; but after going up and down the ladder from sunrise to sunset, for four days, — stopping only for his customary meals, — he went to the Captain, saying: "I can't stand this no more, no how. Guv me arything else, — the rail, the pork-barril, the dungeon, bread and water, — arything but this! Why, my back, and knees, and hams, and calves, and every jint and bone in me, is so sore I can't never walk agin."

The Captain pitied the fellow, and deducted one day, leaving only two to be travelled. But he pleaded for another. "Tuck off another, Captin'," he said, "and I'll tell ye who holped me make the ladder." Here his natural meanness cropped out; even the good-natured Captain was angered; but he only said

to him : "I don't want to know. It is your business
to get out, if you can. I don't blame you for trying,
for I 'd do the same thing myself. But it 's my duty
to keep you in, and to punish you for attempting to
get out. I shall do my duty. Finish the six days ;
and then, if you make another ladder, I 'll give you
twelve." The Captain knew what prisoner he referred
to, and, sending for him, charged him with helping to
make the ladder. " Then the mean critter has telled
on me, Captin'," said the man. " No, he has not," replied the Captain ; " I would n't let him. When you
were a boy in your part of the country, and other
boys told tales about you, what did you do with
them ?" " Whaled 'em like time, Captin'," answered
the man ; " and if ye 'll only shet yer eyes to 't, I 'll
whale him." " I can't allow such things in the
prison," said the Captain ; " and besides, the fellow
will be lame for a fortnight, and would n't be a match
for you in that condition. Let him get limber, and
then — if you don't whale him, I 'll make you walk
the ladder for a month."

The result was, the conscript officer received a
sound thrashing ; and did not commit another act
worthy of punishment for a week. However, on the
day after the Captain related this anecdote, I saw
him going the rounds of the camp with a large board

strapped to his shoulders, on which was painted
"Thief." He had stolen from a comrade, and that
was his punishment.

The Captain was relating to us various instances
in which prisoners had taken the "Air Line" out to
freedom, when a young "native," with a jovial, good-
natured face, and a droll, waggish eye, said to us:
"Speakin' of the 'Air Line' over the fence, stranger,
reminds me of Jake Miles takin' it one night to Chicago. Ye see, Jake was fotched up in a sandy kentry, and never afore seed a pavin'-stone. Well, he
travilled that route one dark night, and made his bed
in a ten-acre lot, with the sky for a kiverlit. It rained
'fore mornin', and Jake woke up, wet through, and
monstrous hungry. Things warn't jist encouragin',
but Jake thought anything better 'n the prison, — and
the fact ar', stranger, though we 'se well treated, and
the Captain 's a monstrous nice man, I myself had
'bout as lief be outside of it as inside. The poet
had this place in his eye, when he said, 'Distance
lends enchantment to the view.' Howsomever, Jake
did n't give up. He put out, determined to see what
this Yankee kentry ar' made of, and soon fotched up
'longside of a baker's cart in Chicago. The driver
was away, and Jake was hungry; so he attempted to
enforce the cornfiscation act; but 'fore he got a single

loaf, a dog sprung out upon him. Jake run, and the dog arter him; and 'fore long the dog cotched him by the trousers, and over they rolled in the mud together. They rolled so fast you could n't tell which from t' other; but Jake felt the pavin'-stones under him, and tried to grab one to subjugate the critter. But the stone would n't come up, — it was fastened down! Finally, Jake got away; and, wet and hungry, and with only one leg to his trousers, tuck a stret line back to camp, declarin' he 'd rather be shot up yere, than go free in a kentry whar they let loose the dogs, and tie up the pavin'-stones!"

"That story will do to tell, my friend," we remark; "but you don't expect us to believe it?"

"B'lieve it!" he answers; "why, stranger, thar 's heaps o' men yere as never seed a pavin'-stone."

That is true, but they are not the ignorant, degraded people they are generally represented to be. The most of them are "poor whites," but so are many people at the North, and in every other country. They have no free schools, and it is that fact which makes the difference between them and our Northern farmers. But even with that disadvantage, at least one half of them can read and write, and many of them are as intelligent as any men you ever spoke with. They are all privates, but there are scores of lawyers, and doctors, and teachers, and clergymen among them. Farther down the lines is Dr. Bronson, who was Demonstrator of Anatomy in the Medical College of Louisiana ; and also a gentleman who was Clerk of the Texas Senate. Though a prisoner, (he has since been released,) this man has done more for the country than at least six Major-Generals you know of. For two days and nights he went through incredible dangers, that he might blot out his record of treason. And he did it nobly. God bless him for it ! Farther on in this book I shall tell you the story, but now we must go on through the prison.

This old man, near upon seventy, with thin, gray hair, only one eye, a ridged, weather-beaten face, and a short jacket and trousers, is "Uncle Ben." He was one of Morgan's men, and was captured while on the raid into Ohio. "You are an old man to be in the war," we say to him. "What led you into it?" "Love of the thing," he answers. "I allers had to be stirrin'. I 'm young enough to ride a nag yet." Talking further with him, we learn that he is a nurse in the hospital, and considers himself well treated. "I never fared better in my life," he says, "but I 'd jist as lief be a ridin' agin."

Most of the men of Morgan's command — and

there are twenty-two hundred in the prison — are
wild, reckless fellows, who went into the war from a
love of adventure, or the hope of plunder. They
would rather fight than eat, and give the keepers
more trouble than all the others in the camp. They
are constantly devising ways of escape ; and one
dark night, about a year ago, nearly a hundred of
them took the Underground Line, and got safely
into Dixie. Here is
a representation of the
route. It was formerly
a fashionable thorough-
fare, but the raising of
the barracks has inter-
cepted the travel, and
broken the hearts of the
stockholders.

As we go on a little far-
ther, a tall fellow, with seedy clothes and a repulsive
countenance, calls to the Captain, "I say, Captin',
I say." The Captain stops, and answers, "Well?"
"I 'se willing to take the oath," says the man. The
Captain's face flushes slightly. He is not angry, —
only indignant ; but the man withers as he answers :
"Willing ! Such a man as *you* talk of being *willing !* You 've shed the best blood in the world, and

you are *willing!* Go down on your marrow-bones, — come back like the prodigal son, — and then the country will take you, — not before." "I 'll do anything that 's wanted," says the man. "Very well; go to the officer, and put down your name," answers the Captain; — adding to us, as we pass on, "That fellow is a great scamp, as thorough a Rebel as any one in the camp."*

"This is my last Sunday here, Captain," says a well-clad, intelligent-looking man, as we go down the lines. "I 'm glad to hear it," replies the Captain; "I thought you 'd come over to our side." In answer to some questions which we put to him, the man explains that he is about enlisting in the Navy. He says he has been "on the fence" for some time, anxious to serve the country, but unwilling to fight against his home and kindred. At last he has compromised the matter by enlisting for an iron-clad; in which, if *his* shots should happen to hit his friends,

---

* But a great many of them were not Rebels. At least one quarter of the whole number confined at Camp Douglas were truly loyal men, who were forced into the Rebel ranks, or had seen the error of their ways, and desired to return to their allegiance. Captain Sponable assured me that he could, in one day, enlist a regiment of a thousand cavalrymen among them, who would be willing to fight for the country with a rope round their necks, — the penalty if taken by the Confederates.

he may be tolerably certain that *theirs* will not hit him! With a full appreciation of his bravery, the Camp Douglas artist has drawn him here, with his back to home and country, and his face to the bounty and the iron-clad.

But from among this army of original characters — and almost all uncultivated men are more or less original — I can particularize no more. Nearly all are stout, healthy, and fine-looking, although there are many mere boys among them. Their clothing is generally badly worn, and scarcely any two are dressed alike. The prevailing material is the reddish-brown homespun so common at the South; but many have on Uncle Sam's coats and trousers, their own having given out, and these being supplied by the government.

Among the scores that I conversed with, not one complained of harsh treatment, and many admitted that they fared much better than at home. The irksomeness of confinement was all that they objected to. Some of them "talked fight," but much the larger number wanted peace at any price. The re-election of Mr. Lincoln they regarded as the death-blow of the Confederacy. Within ten days after the result .of the national election was known among them, nearly eight hundred applied to take the oath of allegiance.

After the Sunday inspection is over, the prisoners go to dinner ; and then such as choose attend divine service, which is performed in the barracks by their own chaplains. These are interesting gatherings, but they are so much like our own religious meetings, that I shall not attempt to describe them. But other things about the prisoners, and about the camp, that may interest you, I shall tell in relating the story of the Rebel prisoner boy, in the next chapter.

THE REBEL PRISONER BOY.

PRISON life is a flat, weary sort of life. Few events occur to break its monotony, and after a time the stoutest frames and the bravest hearts sink under it. If the prisoner were a mere animal, content with eating, drinking, and sleeping, or a twenty-acre lot, — his highest ambition to be bounded by a board fence, — this would not be. But he is a man; he chafes under confinement, and, for want of better employment, his mind feeds upon itself, and gnaws the very flesh off his bones.

The tiresome round of such a life none but a prisoner can know; but I have caught a glimpse of its dull days and weary nights, by looking over the journal of a young man who was confined at Camp Douglas for more than a year. There is little in it to make you laugh: but if you have nothing better to do, suppose you sit with me on the doorstep of this barrack, and trace its noiseless current as it flows, broken here and there by a bubble of hope, or a ripple of fun, on to the dark and silent sea beyond.

He is a slender, dark-haired youth, apparently not more than seventeen or eighteen years of age ; though he has been in the war ever since the 1st of March, 1862. On the afternoon of that day, in the low back room of a store in Knoxville, he was mustered into the service of the Confederate States, which now, thank Heaven, have no existence except in the blood-red history they have caused to be written. Eighteen months later he found himself a prisoner in the jail of the same town ; and, on the 20th of September, 1863, with fifty others, was marched out of it on his way to Camp Douglas. It seemed strange to go a prisoner through streets in which he had passed his lifetime, but such was his experience. Friends gathered round to bid him "farewell," and, I am sorry to say, some Union people to exult over his misfortunes ; but kind voices spoke cheering words, telling him to be of good courage, and to hope for a better time coming, and he went away with a light heart.

A few miles of hard trudging, and he was out of sight of the scenes of his childhood ; and night found the captive company encamped near a little stream, eating their supper of "hard tack" around a fire built in soldier fashion, among a grove of cedars. The boy bathed his tired limbs in the little stream, and then joined his comrades, who, having lighted their pipes, were making acquaintance with the guards around the camp-fire. There they fought their battles over again; held long arguments, which left each party of "the same opinion still," and finally settled the war on principles of justice and equity.

The next morning they were on the march again; and two days later passed through Cumberland Gap, and looked up at the naked cliffs on which they were quartered when forming a part of Zollicoffer's army. This is a wild mountain region, and the scene of a campaign very disastrous to the Confederates. They passed many deserted and dismantled houses, and desolate spots where houses had been, — then only heaps of ashes, and fire-blackened earth, on which the blight of war had fallen.

The next day they came to a little town called Loudon; and there they halted awhile, to rest their weary limbs, and refresh themselves from their long foot-journey. No one gave them any sympathy; but in marching along the street one accosted a lady who was passing. She did not recognize the soldier, and asked where they had met. "I was with Scott on his last raid here," he answered. "Yaw, yaw," shouted several negroes, standing near; "you's on you lass raid now, Mister. Sartin'."

On the following morning they were marched over

Wild-Cat Mountain, — the scene of Zollicoffer's defeat. It is a wild, rocky region, and is appropriately named, as it seems a fit home for only wild-cats and other wild animals. But human beings live there. Before a wretched log shanty, without windows, and with only a ragged hole for a doorway, the weary company saw a half-clad woman and a half-dozen nearly naked and dirt-encrusted children. Before the doorway the woman stood, with a broom in her hand, and, as they passed by, she shook the broomstick at them, and shouted: "O yes! Thet's how ye Rebels orter be, — orter ben long ago." They only laughed; but if you and I had been there, we would not have laughed, — we would have cheered her. Though so very poor, she was richer than they, for she was true to her country; and no doubt she knew that it was such as they who had made her poor, and were even then fighting to make her poorer.

Another day and they reached the "pike," — a hard, macadamized road, — and were transferred into wagons. Many a joke they cracked about "Uncle Sam's coaches"; and they made the woods ring with such songs as "Dixie," and the "Bonnie Blue Flag," but they were truly grateful for the change, for it relieved their weary feet from the tiresome exertion

of marching. Sunset brought them to Camp Nelson; and there they encamped in the woods, and
were soon surrounded with Yankees. It rained hard,
but with his travelling shawl stretched over a stick,
supported on two wooden forks, our prisoner made
a capital tent, and slept dry and soundly until morning. There they remained two days, when they
were marched to Nicholasville, — the end of the railway, — and then their weary march of two hundred
miles was over.

Arriving at Lexington, they were put into a sort
of jail which the renowned freebooter, John Morgan,
used as a slave-pen when he was in the business of
negro-trading. It was a wretched place, and doubtless the noted horse and man stealer would have left
it in better condition, if he had supposed it would so
soon be turned into a hotel for the accommodation
of his friends. A little after dark on the following
day, the train on which they were rolled into the
streets of Louisville. A crowd gathered round, when
they alighted from the cars, and one among it cried
out: "Here they are, — fifty Rebels, and one big
Injun. Rebs, I say, whar der ye come from?

"From Bragg's army," answered one of them.

"Ha! ha!" he shouted. "Whar 's Bragg now?"

"Acting as rear-guard for Rosecrans's army," answered the Rebel; and it was true, for it was just after the battle of Chickamauga. The Union man wisely said nothing more.

They were marched into a prison on Broadway, where they found nearly three hundred of their comrades; and, weary and hungry, turned into the first bunks they could find, too tired even to wait for their suppers. After two days, they were again marched through the streets to the river, where a ferry-boat was in waiting to take them to the Indiana shore. Arrived there, they entered the railway cars which conveyed them to Camp Douglas.

The church bells were sounding twelve on a dark October night, when the train in which they had journeyed all the day halted abreast of the camp, and they heard the gruff summons of the guard: "Turn out! Turn out!" All day long the rain had poured through the roof of the rickety old car, wetting them through and through; and, cold, stiff, and hungry as they were, the summons seemed a cheerful sound, though it welcomed them to a prison. Tumbling out in the mud, and scaling a wall breast-high, they groped their way up the steep bank, and over a couple of fences, and were at the gateway of the camp. Then the ponderous doors rolled back, and for almost the first time in their lives they realized how blessed a thing is freedom. But an extract here and there from the young prisoner's journal will give you a better idea of his life in Camp Douglas than any words of mine.

"Snow," he writes, late in October, "came softly feathering the ground this morning. 'Away down

in Dixie' the golden sunshine of the Indian summer is gilding the hills, and its soft hazy blue is veiling the landscape; but up here in this chilly northern clime we are shivering in the icy grasp of old Winter; and, worse than all, it is my turn to cook!"

"Two months to-day," again he writes, "have I been a prisoner, and a weary long time it seems. The newspapers say exchanges are suspended. If that be true, we are 'in for the war.' A gloomy prospect indeed." — "Christmas has come, — Christmas in prison! How much more we feel our confinement on occasions like this. Reminiscences of many another Christmas come to our minds, and set us to thinking of home and the loved ones there. The consequence is a fit of low spirits. Nearly all of us have tried to prepare some 'good things' from our limited stores in honor of the day. A small 'greenback' has supplied our bunk with a few oysters, and I suspect we are as gay over our modest stew, eaten from a tin pan with an iron spoon, as many an 'outsider' is over his splendid feast of champagne and 'chicken fixins.'"—"But Christmas has gone, and yet no hope of exchange! How long, O Lord! How long!"

"No prisoner at Camp Douglas will forget New-Year's Day, 1864, if he should live a thousand years. To say it was cold does not express it at all. It was frightfully, awfully cold. When I awoke this morning the roof and rafters were covered with frost, and in many places icicles, two or three inches long, hung down from the beams. They were our breath which had congealed during the night. The frost inside was heavier than any I ever saw outside on a winter day in 'Dixie.' A few of our men went down to head-quarters, and, on returning, one had his ears, and another his ears and nose, frost-bitten. Some of the guards froze at their posts, and one sentinel

fell down near our barrack, frozen, — not to death, but very near to it. A few of us, seeing him fall, took him into our quarters, thus saving his life. People who have always lived here say they never experienced such weather. The mercury in the thermometer fell to forty degrees below zero."

"The weather has moderated, and to-day we have been reminded that the earth once was green. A load of hay has invaded the camp, to fill our bunks, and stir our blood with a little frolic. A rich scene occurred in dividing it among the barracks. Before the wagon reached the head of the Square, out poured the 'Rebels,' and, with the war-cry of 'Hay! Hay!' they charged upon it, and completely checked its progress. In a moment the driver was 'nowhere.' One fellow secured an armful, and started for his barrack, but before he reached the outside of the crowd it was reduced to a wisp of straw. Then three or four, more enterprising than the rest, climbed to the top of the load, and soon it was covered with men. By this time the driver, armed with whip and pitchfork, fought his way back, and, mounting the cart, began to clear it. One he pushed off, another required a poke from the pitchfork; but all secured an armful of the hay before they gave up the ground. The driver then tossed the remainder off, and, as each wisp fell, a score of hands were raised to catch it. The boys 'went in' for fun, more than for hay, and scarcely one was lucky enough to fill his bunk."

Farther on, the prisoner writes : " Last night several men in 'White Oak Square' attempted to escape by scaling the fence. Some succeeded, but one was shot. To-day I hear that he will die. . . . . He is dead."

The poor fellows who attempted to escape, and did not succeed, were punished in various ways, and some

of the ways were of the most ludicrous character. There is a grim sort of humor about the keeper, which seems to delight in odd and comical modes of punishment for the refractory prisoners. They do no harm, and are a far more effectual means of restraint than the old-fashioned confinement in a dungeon, with its accompanying diet of bread and water. One of these modes is "riding on a rail," which, ever since Saxe wrote about it, most people have thought a pleasant way to travel. Many a light-hearted "native" has laughed at it; but a half-hour's ride has made him long for "a chance afoot," or even a lift on a broomstick. Another mode is mounting the pork-barrel. In this the prisoner is  perched upon a barrel, and left to stand, a longer or shorter time, in the centre of the prison-yard, where he is naturally "the observed of all observers." If he has any shame about him, he soon concludes that "the post of honor is a private station." Still another mode is drawing a ball and chain about the camp. The culprit lights his pipe, assumes a nonchalant air, and tries to make you think he is having an easy time of it; but look at him when half a day on his travels, and his face will tell you that he never again will make a dray-horse of himself.

But to return to the prisoner's journal. Winter goes, and spring comes, sunny and genial, remind-ing him of the pleasant May time at home; but with it comes no hope of release. Time drags more heavily than before, an¹ every page bears some ː ch sentences as these: 'I am wearied out with this hopeless impris-onment." "Prison life is beginning to tell upon me. Fits of low spirits come oftener than they did." "It seems as if the entan-glement in regard to exchange would *never* end." "For a little while last night I was in heaven. In my dreams I was exchanged, and at home. But I awoke, and the familiar roof and straw-stuffed bunk told me I was still in 'durance vile.' O Dixie! how I long for a glimpse of your sunny hills."

Farther on he writes: "Two years ago to-day I was mustered into the service of the Confederate States. I wondered then what would be the con-dition of things when our twelve months was out. All thought the war would end before our time ex-pired. It is saddening to look back on the changes that have occurred since then. A Federal army holds my native town, and our company, its officers, and myself are all occupants of a Northern prison. When will all this end?" .

At last summer comes, with its scorching days and sultry nights. The snowy winter and the rainy spring were hard to bear, but the summer is even harder, and is made less endurable, he writes, "by a scarcity of water. The hydrants have either

stopped running altogether, or run only in small dribblets. Forming in line," he says, "with our buckets in our hands, we watch them, often for half a day, before we get the needful supply."

And so the weary days wear away, till at last it

11 *

seems that Time has stopped his car, waiting the issue of the dreadful war between brothers. But Time is not waiting. Still his terrible scythe is mowing, — mowing down the young and strong, and bearing them from the prisoner's sight forever. Thirteen have been borne away, — thirteen out of a company of fifty! As each one goes, the boy's face grows paler, his smile fainter, his step more feeble. May not his own turn soon come to follow? But hark! the bells are ringing and the cannon firing, even while he asks the question. He stops in his moody walk, and earnestly listens. Clear and loud the bells ring out, "Richmond has fallen. The great Rebellion is over!" He sends up a wild, glad shout, for now he is free. The country he has sought to destroy rewards him with pardon! Never again, we may be sure, will he lift his hand against it, — never again fight against his own freedom.

THE GREAT CONSPIRACY.

HAVING told you all about the great prison, and its prisoners, I will now tell you of the great conspiracy which the Rebels formed to capture the prison, liberate the prisoners, and set the whole West aflame with Rebellion.

All of you have heard of a famous Report, published by Judge Holt, — Judge Advocate General of the United States, — just prior to the last national election, which disclosed the existence of a widespread conspiracy at the West, having for its object the overthrow of the Union. This conspiracy, the Report stated, had a military organization, with a commander-in-chief, general, and subordinate officers, and five hundred thousand enrolled members, all bound to a blind obedience to the orders of their superiors, and pledged to "take up arms against any government found waging war against a people endeavoring to establish a government of their own choice."

The organization, it was stated, was in every way hostile to the Union, and friendly to the so-called

Confederacy; and the principal objects which Judge Holt said it aimed to accomplish were "a general rising in Missouri," and a similar "rising in Indiana, Ohio, Illinois, and Kentucky, in co-operation with a Rebel force which was to invade the last-named State."

A great many good people, when the Report appeared, shook their heads, and pronounced it an election falsehood; but startling and incredible as it seemed, it told nothing but the truth, and it did not tell the whole truth. It omitted to state that the organization was planned in Richmond; that its operations were directed by Jacob Thompson, — once Mr. Buchanan's Secretary of the Interior, but then a noted Rebel, — who was in Canada for that purpose; and that wholesale robbery, arson, and midnight assassination were among its designs.

The point marked out for the first attack was Camp Douglas, about which I have told you in previous chapters. The eight thousand Rebel soldiers confined there, being liberated and armed, were to be joined by the Canadian refugees and Missouri "Butternuts," who were to effect their release, and the five thousand and more members of the treasonable order resident in Chicago. This force of nearly twenty thousand men would be a nucleus about which the conspirators in other parts of Illinois could gather; and, being joined by the prisoners liberated from other camps, and members of the order from other States, would form an army a hundred thousand strong. · So fully had everything been foreseen and provided for, that the leaders expected to gather and organize this vast body of men within the space of a fortnight! The United States could bring into the field no force capable of withstanding the progress of such an army. The consequences would be, that the whole character of the war would be changed; its theatre would be shifted from the Border to the heart of the Free States; and Southern independence, and the beginning of that process of separation among the Northern States so confidently counted on by the Rebel leaders at the outbreak of hostilities, would have followed.

What saved the nation from being drawn into this whirlpool of ruin? Nothing but the cool brain, sleepless vigilance, and wonderful sagacity of one man, — a young officer never read of in the newspapers, — removed from field duty because of disability, but commissioned, I verily believe, by a good Providence to ferret out and foil this deeper-laid, wider-spread, and more diabolical conspiracy than any that darkens the page of history. Other men — and women, too

— were instrumental in dragging the dark iniquity to light; but they failed to fathom its full enormity, and to discover its point of outbreak. ˙ He did that; and he throttled the tiger when about to spring, and so deserves the lasting gratitude of his country. How he. did it I propose to tell you in this chapter. It is a marvellous tale; it will read more like romance than history; but, calling to mind what a good man once said to me, "Write the truth; let people doubt, if they will," I shall tell you the story.

There is nothing remarkable in the appearance of this young man. Nearly six feet high, he has an erect military carriage, a frank, manly face, and looks every inch a soldier, — such a soldier as would stand up all day in a square hand-to-hand fight with an open enemy; but the keenest eye would detect in him no indication of the crafty genius which delights to follow the windings of wickedness when burrowing in the dark. But if not a Fouché or a Vidocq, he is certainly an able man; for, in a section where able men are as plenty as apple-blossoms in June, he was chosen to represent his district in the State Senate, and, entering the army a subaltern officer, rose, before the Battle of Perryville, to the command of a regiment. At that battle a Rebel bullet entered his shoulder, and crushed the bones of his right elbow.

This disabled him for field duty, and so it came about that he assumed the light blue of the veterans, and on the second day of May, 1864, succeeded General Orme in command of the military post at Chicago. Here is his picture, and I think it will show you that my description of him is correct.

When fairly settled in the low-roofed shanty which stands, — as you will see by looking at the picture on a previous page, — a sort of mute sentry, over the front gateway of Camp Douglas, the new Commandant, as was natural, looked about him. He found the camp had a garrison of but two regiments of veteran reserves, numbering, all told, only seven hundred men fit for duty. This small force was guarding more than eight thousand Rebel prisoners, one third of whom were Texas rangers, and guerrillas who had served under Morgan, — wild, reckless characters, fonder of a fight than of a dinner, and ready for any enterprise, however desperate, that held out the smallest prospect of freedom. To add to the seeming insecurity, nearly every office in the camp was filled with these prisoners. They served out rations and distributed clothing to their comrades, dealt out ammunition to the guards, and even kept the records in the quarters of the Commandant. In fact, the prison was in charge of the prisoners, not the prisoners in charge of the prison. This state of things underwent a sudden change. With the exception of a very few, whose characters recommended them to peculiar confidence, all were at once placed where they belonged, — on the inner side of the prison fence.

A post-office was connected with the camp, and this next received the Commandant's attention. Everything about it appeared to be regular. A vast number of letters came and went, but they all passed unsealed, and seemed to contain nothing contraband. Many of them, however, were short epistles, on long pieces of paper, a curious circumstance among correspondents with whom stationery was scarce and greenbacks not over-plenty. One sultry day in June, the Commandant builded a fire, and gave these letters a warming; and lo! presto! the white spaces broke out into dark lines breathing thoughts blacker than the fluid that wrote them. Corporal Snooks whispered to his wife, away down in Texas, "The forthe of July is comin', Sukey, so be a man; fur I'm gwine to celerbrate. I'm gwine up loike a rocket, ef I does come down loike a stick." And Sergeant Blower said to John Copperhead of Chicago, "Down in 'old Virginny' I used to think the fourth of July a humbug, but this prison has made me a patriot. Now I'd like to burn an all-fired sight of powder, and if you help, and God is willing, I shall do it." In a similar strain wrote half a score of them.

Such patriotism seemed altogether too wordy to be genuine. It told nothing, but it darkly hinted at dark events to come. The Commandant bethought him that the Democratic Convention would assemble on the 4th of July; that a vast multitude of people would congregate at Chicago on that occasion; and that, in so great a throng, it would be easy for the clans to gather, attack the camp, and liberate the prisoners. "Eternal vigilance is the price of liberty," and the young Commandant was vigilant. Soon Prison-Square received a fresh instalment of prisoners. They were genuine "Butternuts," out at the toes, out at the knees, out at the elbows, out everywhere, in fact, and of everything but their senses. Those they had snugly about them. They fraternized with Corporal Snooks, Sergeant Blower, and others of their comrades, and soon learned that a grand pyrotechnic display was arranged to come off on Independence-day. A huge bonfire was to be built outside, and the prisoners were to salute the old flag, but not with blank cartridges.

But who was to light the outside bonfire? That the improvised "Butternuts" failed to discover, and the Commandant set his own wits to working. He soon ascertained that a singular organization existed in Chicago. It was called "The Society of the Il-lini," and its object as set forth by its printed con-stitution, was "the more perfect development of the literary, scientific, moral, physical, and social welfare of the conservative citizens of Chicago." The Com-mandant knew a conservative citizen whose develop-ment was not altogether perfect, and he recommended him to join the organization. The society needed recruits and initiation-fees, and received the new member with open arms. Soon he was deep in the outer secrets of the order; but he could not pene-trate its inner mysteries. Those were open to only an elect few who had already attained to a "perfect development" — of villany. He learned enough, however, to verify the dark hints thrown out by the prisoners. The society numbered some thousands of members, all fully armed, thoroughly drilled, and impatiently waiting a signal to ignite a mine deeper than that which exploded in front of Petersburg.

But the assembling of the Chicago Convention was postponed to the 29th of August, and the 4th of July passed away without the bonfire and the fire-works.

The Commandant, however, did not sleep.   He
still kept his wits a-working ; the bogus "Butternuts"
still ate prisoners rations ; and the red flame still
brought out black thoughts on the white letter-paper.
Quietly the garrison was reinforced, quietly increased
vigilance was enjoined upon the sentinels ; and the
tranquil, assured look of the Commandant told no
one that he was playing with ·hot coals on a barrel
of gunpowder.

So July rolled away into August, and the Commandant sent a letter giving his view of the state˙of
things to his commanding general.   This letter has
fallen into my hands, and, as might sometimes makes
right, I shall copy a portion of it.   It is dated August 12, 1864, and, in the formal phrase customary
among military men, begins : —

"I have the honor respectfully to report, in relation to the supposed organization at Toronto, Canada, which was to come here in squads, then com-
bine, and attempt to rescue the prisoners of war at
Camp Douglas, that there is an armed organization
in this city of five thousand men, and that the rescue
of our prisoners would be the signal for a general
insurrection in Indiana and Illinois. . . . .

"There is little, if any, doubt that an organization
hostile to the Government and secret in its workings

and character exists in the States of Indiana and Illinois, and that this organization is strong in numbers. It would be easy, perhaps, at any crisis in public affairs to push this organization into acts of open disloyalty, if its leaders should so will. . . . .

"Except in cases of considerable emergency, I shall make all communications to your head-quarters on this subject by mail."

These extracts show, that, seventeen days before the assembling of the Chicago Convention, the Commandant had become convinced that mail-bags were safer vehicles of communication than telegraph-wires ; that five thousand armed traitors were then domiciled in Chicago ; that they expected to be joined by a body of Rebels from Canada ; that the object of the combination was the rescue of the prisoners at Camp Douglas ; and that success in that enterprise would be the signal for a general uprising throughout Indiana and Illinois. Certainly, this was no little knowledge to gain by two months' burrowing in the dark. But the conspirators were not fools. They had necks which they valued. They would not plunge into open disloyalty until some "crisis in public affairs" should engage the attention of the authorities, and afford a fair chance of success. Would the assembling of the Convention be such a crisis? was now the question.

The question was soon answered. About this time Lieutenant-Colonel B. H. Hill, commanding the military district of Michigan, received a missive from a person in Canada who represented himself to be a major in the Confederate service. He expressed a readiness to disclose a dangerous plot against the Government, provided he were allowed to take the oath of allegiance, and rewarded according to the value of his information. The Lieutenant-Colonel read the letter, tossed it aside, and went about his business. No good, he had heard, ever came out of Nazareth. Soon another missive, of the same purport, and from the same person, came to him. He tossed this aside also, and went again about his business. But the Major was a Southern Yankee, — the "cutest" sort of Yankee. He had something to sell, and was bound to sell it, even if he had to throw his neck into the bargain. Taking his life in his hand he crossed the frontier; and so it came about, that, late one night, a tall man, in a slouched hat, rusty regimentals, and immense jack-boots, was ushered into the private apartment of the Lieutenant-Colonel at Detroit. It was the Major. He had brought his wares with him. They had cost him nothing, except some small sacrifice of such trifling matters as honor, fraternal feeling, and good faith

towards brother conspirators, whom they might send
to the gallows; but they were of immense value,
— would save millions of money and rivers of loyal
blood. So the Major said, and so the Lieutenant-
Colonel thought, as, coolly, with his cigar in his
mouth, and his legs over the arm of his chair, he
drew the important secrets from the Rebel officer.
Something good might, after all, come out of Nazareth. The Lieutenant-Colonel would trust the fellow, — trust him, but pay him nothing, and send him
back to Toronto to worm out the whole plan from
the Rebel leaders, and to gather the whole details of
the projected expedition. But the Major knew with
whom he was dealing. He had faith in Uncle Sam,
and he was right in having it; for, truth to tell, if
Uncle Sam does not always pay, he can always be
trusted.

It was not long before the Major reappeared with
his budget, which he duly opened to the Lieutenant-
Colonel. Its contents were interesting, and I will
give them to you as the Union officer gave them to
the General commanding the Northern Department.
His communication is dated August 16, 1864. It
says : —

"I have the honor to report that I had another
interview last evening with Major ——, whose dis-

closures in relation to a Rebel plot for the release of the prisoners at Camp Douglas I gave you in my letter of the 8th instant. I have caused inquiries to be made in Canada about Major ——, and understand that he does possess the confidence of the Rebel agent, and that his statements are entitled to respect.

"He now informs me that he proceeded to Toronto, as he stated he would when I last saw him; that about two hundred picked men, of the Rebel refugees in Canada, are assembled at that place, who are armed with revolvers and supplied with funds and transportation-tickets to Chicago; and that already one hundred and fifty have proceeded to Chicago. That he (Major ——) and the balance of the men are waiting for instructions from Captain Hines, who is the commander of the expedition; that Captain Hines left Toronto last Thursday for Chicago, and at this time is doubtless at Niagara Falls, making the final arrangements with the chief Rebel agents.

"Major —— states that Sanders, Holbrook, and Colonel Hicks were at Toronto, while he was there, engaged in making preparations, etc. The general plan is to accomplish the release of the prisoners at Camp Douglas, and in doing so they will be assisted by an armed organization at Chicago. After being released, the prisoners will be armed, and being joined by the organization in Chicago, will be mounted and proceed to Camp Morton, (at Indianapolis,) and there accomplish a similar object in releasing prisoners. That for months, Rebel emissaries have been travelling through the Northwest; that their arrangements are fully matured; and that they expect to receive large accessions of force from Ohio, Indiana, and Illinois. They expect to destroy the works at Ironton.

"Major ——— says further that he is in hourly expectation of receiving instructions to proceed to Chicago with the balance of the party; that he shall put up at the City Hotel, corner of Lake and State Streets, and register his name as George ———; and that he will then place himself in communication with Colonel Sweet, commanding at Chicago."

The Major did not "put up at the corner of Lake and State Streets," and that relieved the Government from the trouble of estimating the value of his services, and, what is more to be deplored, rendered it impossible for the Commandant to recognize and arrest the Rebel leaders during the sitting of the Chicago Convention. What became of the Major is not known. He may have repented of his good deeds, or his treachery may have been detected and he put out of the way by his accomplices.

It will be noticed how closely the Rebel officer's disclosures accorded with the information gathered through indirect channels by the astute Commandant. When the report was conveyed to him, he may have smiled at this proof of his own sagacity; but he made no change in his arrangements. Quietly and steadily he went on strengthening the camp, augmenting the garrison, and shadowing the footsteps of all suspicious new-comers.

At last the loyal Democrats came together to the great Convention, and with them came Satan also. Bands of ill-favored men, in bushy hair, bad whiskey, and seedy homespun, staggered from the railway-stations, and hung about the street-corners. A reader of Dante or Swedenborg would have taken them for delegates from the lower regions, had not their clothing been plainly perishable, while the devils wear everlasting garments. They had come, they announced, to make a Peace President; but they brandished bowie-knives, and bellowed for war even in the sacred precincts of the Peace Convention. But war or peace, the Commandant was ready for it.

For days reinforcements had poured into the camp, until it actually bristled with bayonets. On every

12

side it was guarded with cannon, and, day and night, mounted men patrolled the avenues to give notice of the first hostile gathering. But there was no gathering. The conspirators were there two thousand strong, with five thousand Illini to back them. From every point of the compass, — from Canada, Missouri, Southern Illinois, Indiana, Ohio, New York, and even loyal Vermont, bloody-minded men had come to give the Peace candidate a red baptism. But "discretion is the better part of valor." The conspirators saw the preparations and disbanded. Not long afterward one of the leaders said to me, "We had spies in every public place, — in the telegraph-office, the camp itself, and even *close by* the Commandant's head-quarters, and knew, hourly, all that was passing. From the observatory, opposite the camp, I myself saw the arrangements for our reception. We outnumbered you two to one, but our force was badly disciplined. Success in such circumstances was impossible; and on the third day of the Convention we announced from head-quarters that an attack at that time was impracticable. It would have cost the lives of hundreds of the prisoners, and perhaps the capture or destruction of the whole of us." So the storm blew over, without the leaden rain, and its usual accompaniment of thunder and lightning.

A dead calm followed, during which the Illini slunk back to their holes ; the prisoners took to honest ink ; the bogus "Butternuts" walked the streets clad like Christians, and the Commandant went to sleep with only one eye open. So the world rolled around into November.

The Presidential election was near at hand, — the great contest on which hung the fate of the Republic. The Commandant was convinced of this, and wanted to marshal his old constituents for the final struggle between Freedom and Despotism. He obtained a furlough to go home and mount the stump for the Union. He was about to set out, his private secretary was ready, and the carriage waiting at the gateway, when an indefinable feeling took possession of him, holding him back, and warning him of coming danger. It would not be shaken off, and reluctantly he postponed the journey till the morrow. Before the morrow facts were developed which made his presence in Chicago essential to the safety of the city and the lives of the citizens. The snake was scotched, not killed. It was preparing for another and a deadlier spring. In the following singular and providential way he received warning of the danger.

On the 2d of November, a well-known citizen of

St. Louis, openly a Secessionist, but secretly a loyal man, and acting as a detective for the Government, left that city in pursuit of a criminal. He followed him to Springfield, traced him from there to Chicago, and on the morning of November 4th, about the hour the Commandant had the singular impression I have spoken of, arrived in the latter city. He soon learned that the bird had again flown.

"While passing along the street," (I now quote from his report to the Provost-Marshal General of Missouri,) "and trying to decide what course to pursue, — whether to follow this man to New York, or return to St. Louis, — I met an old acquaintance, a member of the order of 'American Knights,' who informed me that Marmaduke was in Chicago. After conversing with him awhile, I started up the street, and about one block farther on met Dr. E. W. Edwards, a practising physician in Chicago, (another old acquaintance,) who asked me if I knew of any Southern soldiers in town. I told him I did; that Marmaduke (a Rebel officer) was there. He seemed very much astonished, and asked how I knew. I told him. He laughed, and then said that Marmaduke was at his house, under the assumed name of Burling, and mentioned, as a good joke, that he had a British passport, *vised* by the United States Consul

under that name. · I gave Edwards my card to hand
to Marmaduke (who was another 'old acquaintance'),
and told him I was stopping at the Briggs House.

"That same evening I again met Dr. Edwards
on the street, going to my hotel. He said Marmaduke desired to see me, and I accompanied him to
his house." There, in the course of a long conversation, "Marmaduke told me that he and several
Rebel officers were in Chicago to co-operate with
other parties in releasing the ·prisoners of Camp
Douglas, and other prisons, and inaugurating a Rebellion at the North. He said the movement was
under the auspices of the order of 'American Knights'
(to which order the Society of the Illini belonged),
and was to begin operations by an attack on Camp
Douglas on election day."

The detective did not know the Commandant, but
he soon made his acquaintance, and told him the
story. "The young man," he says, "rested his head
upon his hand, and looked as if he had lost his mother." And well he might! A mine had opened at his
feet; with but eight hundred men in the garrison it
was to be sprung upon him. Only seventy hours
were left! What would he not give for twice as
many? In that time he might secure reinforcements. He walked the room for a time in silence,

then, turning to the detective, said, " Do you know where the other leaders are?" — "I do not." — "Can't you find out from Marmaduke?" — "I think not. He said what he did say voluntarily. If I were to question him he would suspect me." That was true, and Marmaduke was not of the stuff that betrays a comrade on compulsion. His arrest, therefore, would profit nothing, and might hasten the attack for which the Commandant was so poorly prepared. He sat down and wrote a hurried despatch to his General. Troops! troops! for God's sake, troops! was its burden. Sending it off by a courier, — the telegraph told tales, — he rose, and again walked the room in silence. After a while, with a heavy heart, the detective said, "Good night," and left him.

What passed with the Commandant during the next two hours I do not know. He may have prayed, — he is a praying man, — and there was need of prayer, for the torch was ready to burn millions of property, the knife whetted to take thousands of lives. At the end of the two hours a stranger was ushered into the Commandant's apartments. From the lips and pen of this stranger I have what followed, and I think it may be relied on.

He was a slim, light-haired young man, with fine, regular features, and that indefinable air which denotes good breeding. Recognizing the Commandant by the eagle on his shoulder, he said, "Can I see you alone, sir?" — "Certainly," answered the Union officer, motioning to his secretary to leave the room. "I am a Colonel in the Rebel army," said the stranger, "and have put my life into your hands, to warn you of the most hellish plot in history." — "Your life is safe, sir," replied the other, "if your visit is an honest one. I shall be glad to hear what you have to say. Be seated."

The Rebel officer took the proffered chair, and sat there till far into the morning. I cannot attempt to recount all that passed between them. The written statement the Rebel Colonel has sent to me covers fourteen pages of closely written foolscap; and my interview with him on the subject lasted five hours, by a slow watch. Sixty days previously he had left Richmond with verbal despatches from the Rebel Secretary of War to Jacob Thompson, the Rebel agent in Canada. These despatches had relation to a vast plot, designed to wrap the West in flames, sever it from the East, and secure the independence of the South. Months before, the plot had been concocted by Jeff Davis at Richmond; and in May previous, Thompson, supplied with two hundred and fifty thousand dollars in sterling exchange, had been

sent to Canada to superintend its execution. This
money was lodged in a bank at Montreal, and
had furnished the funds which fitted out the abor-
tive expeditions against Johnson's Island and Camp
Douglas. The plot embraced the order of "American Knights," which was spread all over the West,
and numbered five hundred thousand men, three
hundred and fifty thousand of whom were armed.
A force of twelve hundred men — Canadian refugees, and bushwhackers from Southern Illinois and
Missouri — was to attack Camp Douglas on Tuesday
night, the 8th of November, liberate and arm the
prisoners, and sack Chicago. This was to be the
signal for a general uprising throughout the West,
and for a simultaneous advance by Hood upon Nash-
ville, Buckner upon Louisville, and Price upon St.
Louis. Vallandigham was to head the movement
in Ohio, Bowles in Indiana, and Walsh in Illinois.
The forces were to rendezvous at Dayton and Cincinnati in Ohio, New Albany and Indianapolis in Indiana, and Rock Island, Chicago, and Springfield
in Illinois; and those gathered at the last-named
place, after seizing the arsenal, were to march to aid
Price in taking St. Louis. Prominent Union citizens and officers were to be seized and sent South,
and the more obnoxious of them were to be assassi-

nated. All places taken were to be sacked and destroyed, and a band of a hundred desperate men was organized to burn the larger Northern cities not included in the field of operations. Two hundred Confederate officers, who were to direct the military movements, had been in Canada, but were then stationed throughout the West, at the various points to be attacked, waiting the outbreak at Chicago. Captain Hines, who had won the confidence of Thompson by his successful management of the escape of John Morgan, had control of the initial movement against Camp Douglas; but Colonel Grenfell, assisted by Colonel Marmaduke and a dozen other Rebel officers, was to manage the military part of the operations. All of these officers were at that moment in Chicago, waiting the arrival of the men, who were to come in small squads, over different railroads, during the following three days. The Rebel officer had known of the plot for months, but its atrocious details had come to his knowledge only within a fortnight. They had appalled him; and though he was betraying his friends, and the South which he loved, the humanity in him would not let him rest till he had washed his hands of the horrible crime.

The Commandant listened with nervous interest to the whole of this recital; but when the Southern officer made the last remark, he almost groaned out, — "Why did you not come before?"

"I could not. I gave Thompson my opinion of this, and have been watched. I think they have tracked me here. My life on your streets to-night would n't be worth a bad half-dollar."

"True; but what must be done?"

"Arrest the 'Butternuts' as they come into Chicago."

"That I can do; but the leaders are here with five thousand armed Illini to back them. I must take them. Do you know them?"

"Yes; but I do not know where they are quartered."

And so again the Commandant was unable to arrest the leaders. He must arrest them. It was his only chance of saving the camp, for its little garrison could not defend it against the large force the Rebels could gather; but if the head were gone, the body could do nothing.

At two o'clock the Commandant showed the Rebel officer to his bed, but went back himself and paced the floor until sunrise. In the morning his plan was formed. It was a desperate plan; but desperate circumstances require desperate expedients.

In the prison was a young Texan who had served

on Bragg's staff, and under Morgan in Kentucky, and was therefore acquainted with Hines, Grenfell, and the other Rebel officers. He fully believed in the theory of State Rights, — that is, that a part is greater than the whole, — but was an honest man, who, when his word was given, could be trusted. One glance at his open, resolute face showed that he feared nothing ; that he had, too, that rare courage which delights in danger, and courts heroic enterprise from pure love of peril. Early in the war he had encountered Colonel De Land, a former Commandant of the post, on the battle-field, and taken him prisoner. A friendship then sprang up between the two, which, when the tables were turned, and the captor became the captive, was not forgotten. Colonel De Land made him chief clerk in the medical department of the prison, and gave him every possible freedom. At that time it was the custom to allow citizens free access to the camp ; and among the many good men and women who came to visit and aid the prisoners was a young woman, the daughter of a well-known resident of Chicago. She met the Texan, and a result as natural as the union of hydrogen and oxygen followed. But since Adam courted Eve, who ever heard of wooing going on in a prison? "It is not exactly the thing," said Colonel De Land ; "had you not better pay your addresses at the lady's house, like a gentleman?" A guard accompanied the prisoner; but it was shrewdly guessed that he stayed outside, or paid court to the girls in the kitchen.

This was the state of things when the present Commandant took charge of the camp. He learned the facts, studied the prisoner's face, and remembered that he, too, once went a-courting. As he walked his room that Friday night, he bethought him of the Texan. Did he love his State better than he loved his affianced wife? The Commandant would test him. He sent for him; told him of the danger surrounding the camp, and proposed that he should escape from the prison, (to give the Rebels confidence in him,) and ferret out and entrap the leaders. The Texan heard him through in silence, then, shaking his head, said, "But I shall betray my friends! Can I do that in honor?"

"Did you ask that question when you betrayed your country?" answered the Commandant.

"Let me go from camp for an hour. Then I will give you my decision," said the Texan, after a moment's reflection.

"Very well," replied the Commandant, and, unattended, the Texan left the prison.

He wanted to consult with the young woman to

whom he was attached. What passed between them during that hour I do not know, and could not tell you if I did know, — for I am not writing romance, but history. However, without lifting the veil on things sacred, I can say that her last words were, " Do your duty. Blot out your record of treason." God bless her for saying them! and let "Amen" be said by every American!

On his return to camp, the Texan merely said, " I will do it," and the details of the plan were talked over. How to manage to escape from the prison was the query of the Texan. The Commandant's brain is fertile. An adopted citizen, in the scavenger line, makes periodical visits to the camp in the way of his business. Him the Commandant sends for, and proposes he shall aid the Texan.

"Arrah, yer Honor," the Irishman says, " I ha'n't a tr-raitor. Bless yer beautiful sowl! I love the kintry; and besides, it might damage me good name and me purty prefession."

He is assured that his good name will be all the better for a few weeks' dieting in a dungeon, and — did not the same thing make Harvey Birch immortal?

Half an hour before sunset the scavenger comes into camp with his wagon. He fills it with dry bones, broken bottles, decayed food, and the rubbish of the prison; and down below, under a blanket, he stows away the Texan. A hundred comrades gather round to shut off the gaze of the guard: but outside is the real danger. He has to pass two gates, and run the gantlet of half a dozen sentinels. His wagon is fuller than usual; and the late hour — it is now after sunset — will of itself excite suspicion. It might test the pluck of a braver man; for the sentries' bayonets are fixed, and their guns at the half-trigger; but he reaches the outer gate in safety. Now, St. Patrick help him! for he needs all the impudence of an Irishman. The gate rolls back; the Commandant stands nervously by, but a sentry cries out, "You can't pass; it's agin orders. No wagins kin go out arter drum-beat."

"Arrah, don't be a fool! Don't be afther obstructin' a honest man's business," answers the Irishman, pushing on into the gateway.

The soldier is vigilant, for his officer's eye is on him.

"Halt!" he cries again, "or I'll fire!"

"Fire! Waste yer powder on yer friends, like the bloody-minded spalpeen ye are!" says the scavenger, cracking his whip, and moving forward.

It is well he does not look back. If he should,

he might be melted to his own soap-grease. The
sentry's musket is levelled; he is about to fire, but
the Commandant roars out, "Don't shoot!" and
the old man and the old horse trot off into the twi-
light.

Not an hour later, two men, in big boots, slouched
hats, and brownish butternuts, come out of the Commandant's quarters. With muffled faces and hasty
strides, they make their way over the dimly lighted
road into the city. Pausing, after a while, before a
large mansion, they crouch down among the shadows. It is the house of the Grand Treasurer, of
the Order of American Knights, and into it very
soon they see the Texan enter. He has been sent
there by the Commandant to learn the whereabouts
of the Rebel leaders. The good man knows him well,
and rejoices greatly over his escape. He orders up
the fatted calf, and soon it is on the table, steaming
hot, and done brown in the roasting. When the meal
is over, they discuss a bottle of Champagne and the
situation. The Texan cannot remain in Chicago,
the good man says, for there he will surely be detected. He must be off to Cincinnati by the first
train; and he will arrive in the nick of time, for
warm work is daily expected. Has he any money
about him? No, the Texan answers, he has left it

behind with his Sunday clothes, in the prison. He must have funds, the worthy gentleman thinks, but he can lend him none, for he is a loyal man; of course he is! was he not the "people's candidate" for Governor? But no one ever heard of a woman being hanged for treason. With this he nods to his wife, who opens her purse, and tosses the Texan a roll of greenbacks. They are honest notes, for an honest face is on them. At the end of an hour good night is said, and the Texan goes out to find a hole to hide in. Down the street he hurries, the long, dark shadows following.

He enters the private door of a public house, speaks a magic word, and is shown to a room in the upper story. Three low, prolonged raps on the wall, and — he is among them. They are seated about a small table, on which is a plan of the prison. One is about forty-five, — a tall, thin man, with a wiry frame, a jovial face, and eyes which have the wild, roving look of the Arab's. He is dressed after the fashion of English sportsmen, and his dog — a fine gray bloodhound — is stretched on the hearth-rug near him. He looks a reckless, desperate character, and has an adventurous history.* In battle he

* See Freemantle's "Three Months in the Southern States," p. 148.

is said to be a thunderbolt, — lightning harnessed and inspired with the will of a devil. He is just the character to lead the dark, desperate expedition on which they are entered. It is St. Leger Grenfell.

At his right sits another tall, erect man, of about thirty, with large, prominent eyes, and thin, black hair and moustache. He is of dark complexion, has a sharp, thin nose, a small, close mouth, a coarse, harsh voice, and a quick, boisterous manner. His face tells of dissipation, and his dress shows the dandy; but his deep, clear eye, and pale, wrinkled forehead denote a cool, crafty intellect.* This is the notorious Captain Hines, the right-hand man of Morgan, and the soul and brains of the conspiracy. The rest are the meaner sort of villains. I do not know how they looked; and if I did, they would not be worth describing.

Hines and Grenfell spring to their feet, and grasp the hand of the Texan. They know his reckless, indomitable courage, and he is a godsend to them; sent to do what no man of them is brave enough to do, — lead the attack on the front gateway of the prison. So they affirm, with great oaths, as they sit down, spread out the map, and explain to him the plan of operations.

* Detective's description.

Two hundred Rebel refugees from Canada, they say, and a hundred "Butternuts" from Fayette and Christian Counties, have already arrived; many more from Kentucky and Missouri are coming; and by Tuesday they expect a thousand or twelve hundred desperate men, armed to the teeth, to be in Chicago. Taking advantage of the excitement of election-night, they propose, with this force, to attack the camp and prison. It will be divided into five parties. One squad, under Grenfell, will be held in reserve a few hundred yards from the main body, and will guard the large number of guns already provided to arm the prisoners. Another — command of which is offered to the Texan — will assault the front gateway, and engage the attention of the eight hundred troops quartered in Garrison Square. The work of this squad will be dangerous, for it will encounter a force four times its strength, well-armed and supplied with artillery; but it will be speedily relieved by the other divisions. Those, under Marmaduke, Colonel Robert Anderson of Kentucky, and Brigadier-General Charles Walsh of Chicago, Commander of the American Knights, will simultaneously assail three sides of Prison Square, break down the fence, liberate the prisoners, and, taking the garrison in rear, compel a general surrender. This accomplished, small parties will be despatched to cut the telegraph-wires, and seize the railway-stations; while the main body, reinforced by the eight thousand and more prisoners, will march into the city and rendezvous in Court-House Square, which will be the base of further operations.

The first blow struck, the insurgents will be joined by the five thousand Illini (American Knights), and, seizing the arms of the city, — six brass field-pieces and eight hundred Springfield muskets, — and the arms and ammunition stored in private warehouses, will begin the work of destruction. The banks will be robbed, the stores gutted, the houses of loyal men plundered, and the railway-stations, grain-elevators, and other public buildings burned to the gound. To facilitate this latter design, the water-plugs have been marked, and a force detailed to set the water running. In brief, the war will be brought home to the North; Chicago will be dealt with like a city taken by assault, given up to the flames, the sword, and the brutal passions of a drunken soldiery. On it will be wreaked all the havoc, the agony, and the desolation which three years of war have heaped upon the South; and its upgoing flames will be the torch that shall light a score of other cities to the same destruction.

It was a diabolical plan, conceived far down amid the thick blackness, and brought up by the arch-fiend himself, who sat there, toying with the hideous thing, and with his cloven foot beating a merry tune on the death's-head and cross-bones under the table.

As he concludes, Hines turns to the new-comer, "Well, my boy, what do you say? Will you take the post of honor and of danger?"

The Texan draws a long breath, and then, through his barred teeth, blurts out, "I will!"

On those two words hang thousands of lives, millions of money!

"You are a trump!" shouts Grenfell, springing to his feet. "Give us your hand upon it!"

A general hand-shaking follows, and during it, Hines and another man announce that their time is up: "It is nearly twelve. Fielding and I never stay in this d——d town after midnight. You are fools, or you would n't."

Suddenly, as these words are uttered, a slouched hat, listening at the keyhole, pops up, moves softly along the hall, and steals down the stairway. It is one of the detectives who have followed the Texan from the prison. Half an hour later he opens the private door of the Richmond House, where all this occurred, looks cautiously around for a moment, and then stalks on towards the heart of the city. The moon is down, the lamps burn dimly, but after him glide the shadows.

In a room at the Tremont House, not far from this time, the Commandant is waiting, when the door opens, and a man enters. His face is flushed, his teeth are clenched, his eyes flashing. He is stirred to the depths of his being. Can he be the Texan?

"What is the matter?" asks the Commandant.

The other sits down, and, as if only talking to himself, tells him. One hour has swept away the fallacies of his lifetime. He sees the Rebellion as it is, — the outbreak and outworking of that spirit which makes hell horrible. Hitherto, that night, he has acted from love, not duty. Now he bows only to the All-Right and the All-Beautiful, and in his heart is that psalm of work, sung by one of old, and by all true men since the dawn of creation: "Here am I, Lord! Send me!"

The first gray of morning is streaking the east, when he goes forth to find a hiding-place. The sun is not up, and the early light comes dimly through the misty clouds, but about him still hang the long, dark shadows. This is a world of shadows. Only in the atmosphere which soon enclosed him is there no night and no shadow.

Soon the Texan's escape is known at the camp, and a great hue and cry follows. Handbills are got out, a reward is offered, and by that Sunday noon his name is on every street-corner. Squads of soldiers and police ransack the city and invade every Rebel asylum. Strange things are brought to light, and strange gentry dragged out of dark closets; but nowhere is found the Texan. The search is well done, for the pursuers are in dead earnest; and, Captain Hines, if you don't trust him now, you are a dunce, with all your astuteness!

So the day wears away and the night cometh. Just at dark a man enters the private door of the Tremont House, and goes up to a room where the Commandant is waiting. He sports a light rattan, wears a stove-pipe hat, a Sunday suit, and is shaven and shorn like unto Samson. What is the Commandant doing with such a dandy? Soon the gas is lighted; and lo, it is the Texan! But who in creation would know him? The plot, he says, thickens. More "Butternuts" have arrived, and the deed will be done on Tuesday night, as sure as Christmas is coming. He has seen his men, — two hundred, picked, and every one clamoring for pickings. Hines, who "carries the bag," is to give him ten thousand greenbacks, to stop their mouths and stuff their pockets, at nine in the morning.

"And to-morrow night we 'll have them, sure ! And, how say you, give *you* shackles and a dungeon?" asks the Commandant, his mouth wreathing with grim wrinkles.

"Anything you like. Anything. to *blot out my record of treason.*"

He has learned the words, — they are on his heart, not to be razed out forever.

When he is gone, up and down the room goes the Commandant, as is his fashion. He is playing a desperate game. The stake is awful. He holds the ace of trumps, — but shall he risk the game upon it? At half past eight he sits down and writes a despatch to his General. In it he says : —

"My force is, as you know, too weak and much overworked, — only eight hundred men, all told, to guard between eight and nine thousand prisoners. I am certainly not justified in waiting to take risks, and mean to arrest these officers, if possible, before morning."

The despatch goes off, but still the Commandant is undecided. If he strikes to-night, Hines may escape, for the fox has a hole out of town, and may keep under cover till morning. He is the king-hawk, and much the Commandant wants to cage him. Besides, he holds the bag, and the Texan will go out of prison a penniless man among strangers. Those ten thousand greenbacks are lawful prize, and should be the country's dower with the maiden. But are not republics grateful? Did not one give a mansion to General McClellan? Ah, Captain Hines, that was lucky for you, for, beyond a doubt, it saved your bacon!

The Commandant goes back to camp, sends for the police, and gets his blue-coats ready. At two o'clock they swoop to the prey, and before daybreak a hundred "birds" are in the talons of the eagle. Such another haul of buzzards and night-hawks never was made since man first went a-hunting.*

* Since the foregoing was written the Commandant's official Report has been published. In reference to these arrests, he says, in a despatch to General Cook, dated Camp Douglas, Nov. 7, 4 o'clock, A. M : —

"Have made during the night the following arrests of Rebel officers, escaped prisoners of war, and citizens in connection with them : —

"Morgan's Adjutant-General, Colonel G. St. Leger Grenfell, in company with J. T. Shanks, [the Texan,] an escaped prisoner of war, at Richmond House ; Colonel Vincent Marmaduke, brother of General Marmaduke ; Brigadier-General Charles Walsh, of the 'Sons of Liberty' ; Captain Cantrill, of Morgan's command ; Charles Traverse (Butternut). Cantrill and Traverse arrested in Walsh's house, in which were found two cartloads of large-size revolvers, loaded and capped, two hundred

At the Richmond House Grenfell was taken in bed with the Texan. They were clapped into irons, and driven off to the prison together. A fortnight later, the Texan, relating these details to the writer,

stands of muskets, loaded, and ammunition. Also seized two boxes of guns concealed in a room in the city. Also arrested Buck Morris, Treasurer of 'Sons of Liberty,' having complete proof of his assisting Shanks to escape, and plotting to release prisoners at this camp.

"Most of these Rebel officers were in this city on the same errand in August last, their plan being to raise an insurrection and release prisoners of war at this camp. There are many strangers and suspicious persons in the city, believed to be guerrillas and Rebel soldiers. Their plan was to attack the camp on election night. All prisoners arrested are in camp. Captain Nelson and A. C. Coventry, of the police, rendered very efficient service.

"B. J. SWEET, *Col. Com.*"

In relation to the general operations I have detailed, the Commandant in this Report writes as follows: —

"Adopting measures which proved effective to detect the presence and identify the persons of the officers and leaders, and ascertain their plans, it was manifest that they had the means of gathering a force considerably larger than the little garrison then guarding between eight and nine thousand prisoners of war at Camp Douglas, and that, taking advantage of the excitement and the large number of persons who would ordinarily fill the streets on election night, they intended to make a night attack on and surprise this camp, release and arm the

13   s

while the Commandant was sitting by at his desk writing, said, "Words cannot describe my relief when those handcuffs were put upon us. At times before, the sense of responsibility almost overpowered me. Then I felt like a man who has just come into a fortune. The wonder to me now is, how the Colonel could have trusted so much to a Rebel."

"Trusted!" echoed the Commandant, looking up from his writing. "I had faith in you; I thought you would n't betray me; but I trusted your own life in your own hands, that was all. Too much was at stake to do more. Your every step was shadowed, from the moment you left this camp till you came back to it in irons. Two detectives were constantly at your back, sworn to take your life if you wavered for half a second."

"Is that true?" asked the Texan in a musing way, but without moving a muscle. "I did n't know it, but I felt it in the air."

prisoners of war, cut the telegraph-wires, burn the railroad depots, seize the banks and stores containing arms and ammunition, take possession of the city, and commence a campaign for the release of other prisoners of war in the States of Illinois and Indiana, thus organizing an army to effect and give success to the general uprising so long contemplated by the 'Sons of Liberty.'"

They were the "shadows" which so long followed him; but they will never follow him more, for now he is living in the sunshine.

At another house where arrests were made, some young "ladies" strongly objected to the search which was being done by Captain Sponable, the "keeper" of the prison. They became very abusive, and one of them forgot that she was a woman; but quietly and courteously the Captain went on with his work, until he found a quantity of newly made cartridges secreted in her bed-chamber. "This," he said, in his pleasant way, holding one of the cartridges up to the lady, "I suppose was meant for the Commandant; and this," holding up another, "for that rascal, the Keeper."

"Yes," she answered, "you 've hit it; and I only wish I could have fired the muskets."

"You don't mean that," he replied, with a pleasant smile; "I know you would n't want to kill me, — I am the Keeper!"

"You!" she exclaimed, "a pleasant gentleman like you! And I have been abusing you all this time, while you have been treating me so kindly! I ask your pardon. I hope you will forgive me!"

This was the power of kindness; and this incident shows that none are altogether bad, — not even the women who make cartridges to murder our soldiers.

In the room at the Richmond House, on the table around which were discussed their diabolical plans, was found a slip of paper, and on it, in pencil, was scrawled the following : —

"COLONEL, — You *must* leave this house *to-night.* Go to the Briggs House.

"J. FIELDING."

Fielding was the assumed name of the Rebel who burrowed with Hines out of town, where not even his fellow-Rebels could find him. Did the old fox scent the danger? Beyond a doubt he did. Another day, and the Texan's life might have been forfeit. Another day, and the camp might have been sprung upon a little too suddenly! So the Commandant was none too soon ; and who that reads what I have written can doubt that through it all he was led and guided by the good Providence that guards his country?

A shiver of genuine horror passed over Chicago when it awoke in the morning. From mouth to mouth the tidings ran ; mothers pressed their babes to their breasts, and fathers clutched their children, appalled at the earthquake which had wellnigh engulfed them. And well they might be affrighted; for no pen can picture the horrors that would have followed the falling of such an avalanche upon the sleeping city. The scene would have had no parallel in savage history.

"One hour of such a catastrophe would destroy the creations of a quarter of a century, and expose the homes of nearly two hundred thousand souls to every conceivable form of desecration."*

And the men of Chicago not only talked, they acted. They went to the polls and voted for the Union; and so told the world what honest Illinois thought of treason.

But the danger was not over. Hines and other Rebel officers were yet at large, and thousands of armed men were still ready for an outbreak at a signal from the leaders. It was election day. Excited crowds thronged the streets, and mingled among them were the bushwhackers. Only a spark was needed to light a conflagration; but the Commandant was equal to the occasion.

The merchants gathered in the Exchange; and he sent them word to arm themselves, and give a musket to every man that could be trusted. Two hundred young men volunteered on the spot, and, under

* Chicago Tribune, November 8, 1864.

Colonel Hough and Adjutant Kimbark, patrolled every street and avenue of the city. All that day, and all that night, and all the next day, they made the weary rounds, — men who had not been in saddle for a twelvemonth, — and then Chicago was saved to the nation.

Meanwhile, searches were going on, and arrests being made hourly. To the "birds" already bagged was soon added another flock of two hundred. The sorriest birds, in red and brown, were emptied into an old church, where they might bewail their sins, and pray for their country. Those of gayer plumage were caged in the dark cells of Camp Douglas. Rare "birds" they were; an embryo Semmes, a city attorney, a would-be sheriff, and a would-be Governor, — would-be assassins all of them.

The President and Secretary of the Illini were arrested, and then the lodges of the worshipful order were visited. The members had met often since the first arrests were made; but they had come together with greater secrecy, redoubled their vigilance, changed their pass-words, and subjected to closer questioning every one who was admitted. They were biding their time, swearing in new members, and preparing to strike with new leaders; but these visits of the soldiers disturbed their dreams, and they scattered like wolves chased by firebrands.

The visit to their principal lodge is thus described by one who was present : " All had departed and the doors were locked, — bolted. The officers rapped, but receiving no answer to their summons, kicked out a panel and entered. An ancient and mouldy odor pervaded the interior, and it was not until the doors and windows were opened, and the blast allowed to sweep through the room, that the atmosphere became endurable. They looked through the apartments and found — one gun. By this time the ancient dame who fills the post of janitress to the building was awakened from a fitful slumber, and wildly rushed to the door of the hall, screaming, 'Fire!' 'Murder!' 'Thieves!' She was finally quieted, and informed of the import of the visit. 'Bejabers,' said she, 'yez ought to hav' bin here the day afore yisterday, an' shure you 'd found lots of fire-arms.' The guard were not there then, and of course the arms were not captured."

The election was over, and on Friday night the loyal men and women of Chicago came together to rejoice in the victory won by the nation. Thousands upon thousands were there ; and, when the Commandant appeared, they sent up cheer after cheer, which resounded through the building till the very walls echoed the enthusiasm of the people. He arose, and when the applause had subsided, said: "I thank you for this cordial greeting. I came here to celebrate with you our great victory. Four years ago, when I entered the army, I cast aside politics, and now know only loyal men and traitors. The loyal men have triumphed; but our victory is not complete. We must crush out every vestige of treason in the North; and, if the Government give me power, I will do my part in the work of subjugation."

He sat down, and the band struck up "My Country." On the following day the Secretary of War sent him the following telegram: "Hold your prisoners and arms captured at all hazards. Your energetic action meets with the approval of this Department."

This telegram was but the echo of the "Well done, good and faithful servant," which arose from every loyal heart all over the nation.

I said, at the outset of this narrative, that it would read more like romance than history; nevertheless, it is true, and true, I believe, in every detail. Its facts were communicated to me by the persons most prominent in the suppression of the conspiracy, within a fortnight after the events occurred; and they have since been confirmed by the "cloud of witnesses" who testified before the military commission which, some months afterwards, tried and convicted the principal conspirators at Cincinnati.

The Commandant, as you will have discovered from the narrative itself, was Colonel B. J. Sweet of Wisconsin. For the important service he rendered the country in this affair he has since been promoted to the rank of Brigadier-General.

While engaged in ferreting out the conspiracy, Colonel Sweet was obliged to expend about one thousand dollars of his private means, in employing detectives to watch the newly arrived "Butternuts," and to unearth the other conspirators, and, no appropriation having been made for such purposes, he was not, at once, refunded this sum by the Government. Hearing of this, the patriotic ladies of the First Baptist Church in Chicago collected the amount, and, investing it in a United States bond, caused its presentation to the Commandant at a public meeting held for the purpose. As the remarks made on that occasion show the estimation in which the citizens of Chicago hold the services of Colonel Sweet, and the great merit and modesty of that officer, I will here repeat a portion of them.

13 *

Hon. George C. Bates was selected by the ladies to make the presentation, and he addressed the Colonel as follows : —

" Referring to the occasion that had summoned him from Camp Douglas, Mr. Bates alluded to his distinguished services, and remarked that some fitting reward for gallantry and patriotism had been won ; that the time had come when justice, duty, and patriotism demanded that the debt should be acknowledged by a whole people saved from ruin, and should be in some slight measure repaid by the endeavors and zeal of Christian ladies, who, as they clasp their little ones to their hearts and kneel around the family altars, night after night, invoke God's choicest blessings on the brave soldier who has, under Providence, saved them, their homes, their families, and their all from the dangers that surrounded and the ruin that encompassed them. Appreciating, as the citizens of Chicago do, the extent of their obligations for your most able and successful efforts for the salvation of the city, their homes, their families, their property, their franchises as men, as voters, and as Unionists, at the instance and request of the ladies of the First Baptist Church of Chicago, they have united to give some form of expression appropriate and enduring of their gratitude to you, and have conferred on me an honor I can never forget, in making me the instrument of the expression of their wishes towards you. Take, then, this bond of the United States, issued from its treasury, under and by virtue of its laws; its value is nominal, compared with the services you have rendered, yet, in any other community it would be considered munificent; and I know that it will ever be inestimable to you, your family and friends. You will value it because its face will always remind you that our Union is strong and rich enough from the purses and coffers of its own people to conquer rebellion, no matter how great; and to continue a war, no matter at what cost, until all who seek to overthrow or destroy it shall yield obedience to its Constitution and laws. You will value it because it will ever remind you that its redemption, and that of the millions upon millions of the like kind, depends upon the perpetuity of our Union; and aside from all patriotic considerations, the pecuniary interests of our whole people demand that its plighted faith shall ever be redeemed. You will value it, because it will always remind you, and your children, and your sainted mother, that it was won by your gallantry, by the highest and holiest of all man's motives, save those that prompt devotion to his God,

— a consecration of your time, your talents, your body, and your blood to your country's service and welfare. You will prize it as a memento of the gratitude and generosity of this great city, whose peculiar characteristics are unequalled energy, bounteous liberality, unflinching loyalty, activity that never slumbers, vigilance that knows no sleeping."

The Commandant modestly replied as follows :—

"Sir, — I thank you for the gracious and eloquent manner in which you have made this presentation, and the fair ladies of the First Baptist Church in whose behalf you have spoken, as well as the generous gentlemen who contributed, for the regard and good will of which they have been pleased to make this valuable gift an expression. [Cheers.]

"Whoever reads the history of these times aright will understand that, throughout the war, whenever victories have been won by courage and endurance, or great interests saved and protected by toil and resolution, by long marches or in answering demands for wearying duty, the burden of sacrifice has been borne by subordinate officers and enlisted men, whose names are seldom written except on the muster-rolls of the army, or in the official lists of dead from disease, or killed and wounded in battle. [Cheers.] And in whatever has been done here of late to foil the en-

emy and protect Chicago, the officers and enlisted
men of the small, patient, willing garrison of Camp
Douglas, rather than myself, deserve gratitude and
commendation. [Cheers.]

"I accept this thousand-dollar bond in the same
spirit in which it is given, and gratefully hope to be
able to send it as an heir-loom down through the gen-
erations which shall come after me, gaining traditional
and intrinsic value as the story of this war is told,
and the government, now assailed, and by which it
was issued, stands firm and proudly against all as-
saults of hatred or foreign intrigue from without, or
of faction or insurrection from within, growing in
wealth, prosperity, population, freedom and national
glory, grandeur and power, through the ages.
[Cheers.]

"Sir, your kind words and the manifestations of
this audience make me feel that henceforward I have
two homes, one in my own beloved and true young
State of Wisconsin, in the little county of Calumet,
which to-night nestles my loved ones from the cold,
under its mantle of snow, where every rivulet and
old rock and tree are dear to me, — among a brave,
honest, and patriotic people, where there are whole
towns in which scarcely an able-bodied man remains
who has not volunteered, been clothed in blue, and

taught the use of arms in defending those free institutions around which the hopes of mankind cluster;
and another home in the hearts of the noble-minded
and generous men and women of this marvellous me-
tropolis of the Northwest, the munificent and loyal
city of Chicago. [Loud and prolonged cheering.]"

This country will ever be safe from all dangers,
whether from within or without, so long as it pro-
duces men so patriotic and self-devoted as the brave
Commandant of Camp Douglas.

The name of the "Texan," you may also have discovered from the lengthy note appended to the narrative, is John T. Shanks. He is a young man of
about twenty-seven, a native of Nacogdoches, Texas,
and, before the war, was the clerk of the Texan
Senate.   He entered the Confederate army as a
Captain in the Eighth Regiment of Texas Rangers,
and, while operating in Kentucky, captured Colonel
De Land, as is related in the narrative. He afterwards resigned his commission, enlisted as a private
under John Morgan, and was made a prisoner while
on the great raid into Ohio. This accounts for his
being at Camp Douglas, where only private soldiers
were confined.

In consideration of the important part he took
in arresting the chief conspirators, the Rebel agents

in Canada offered a thousand dollars in gold for his assassination ; and our Government conferred on him the commission of Captain in the United States Army. In August, 1865, he was stationed, with his regiment, at Camp Rankin, in Colorado Territory, and, at that time, wrote me a letter which is so characteristic of the man, that, though it was meant for no eye but mine, I am tempted to quote a portion of it. In it he says : " The assistance I rendered the military authorities in detecting the Rebel officers was prompted solely by patriotic principle, and not by the hope of any future aggrandizement. By doing what I did, I have incurred the ill-will of many thousands whom I regard as worse enemies to the country than the bitterest Rebels ever confined at Camp Douglas. I feel *very grateful* for the honor conferred on me, — the commission of Captain in the United States army, — and also proud that I again possess the confidence and good will of the best government that ever existed ; and my pride and ambition will ever be to show, *by my acts*, that I merit its confidence."

He was an honest Rebel, and is now an honest Union man ; and I know every one of my readers will wish him a long and happy life with the noble woman he so bravely won.

The real name of the St. Louis detective who so opportunely arrived in Chicago is William Jones, though he passed, among the Rebels, as Doctor Bledsaw. I did not meet him personally; and the account I give in the narrative of his interviews with Marmaduke and the Commandant was taken from a written statement made by him to the Provost Marshal General of Missouri, which statement is now in my possession.

The Rebel officer who communicated with Lieutenant-Colonel Hill, at Detroit, was a Major Young. He was concerned in the St. Alban's raid; and, after this narrative was written, was mentioned in the public prints as acting with the Rebels in Canada; and, if accounts are true, played false with both his friends and his enemies. He was actuated only by sordid motives; but his baseness, by the overruling Hand, was made to benefit the country he was willing to serve, or to sell, for " thirty pieces of silver."

The other Rebel officer who gave the important information to the Commandant, on the eve of the intended attack on the camp, was Lieutenant-Colonel Maurice Langhorn, of the Thirtieth Regiment of Arkansas Infantry. His home was at Marysville, Bourbon County, Kentucky; and twice during the war he was a candidate for the office of Representative

in the Confederate Congress from his native district;
but was defeated, because not sufficiently radical on
the question of Secession. He is widely and very
favorably known in Kentucky ; and it was he who
communicated to Secretary Seward the Rebel plot
to burn the principal Northern cities. I have heard
from him but once since I met him in Chicago. He
was then at Camp Douglas, in danger of his life, —
a price having been set on it by the Canadian Rebels.
With his present whereabouts I am not acquainted.

The name of the scavenger who, at the risk of
disgrace and imprisonment, aided the Texan to escape from the. prison, I do not remember; and I
regret that I do not, for he is deserving of as much
honor as those who acted the more important parts
in this wonderful drama. He is a noble Irishman ;
and I never meet an Irish scavenger but I feel like
lifting my hat to him, out of respect and gratitude
to his brother Irishman and scavenger, who did so
great a service to his adopted country at Camp
Douglas.

On a railway in Michigan, about a year ago, I
met a man who. said to.me : " Sir, I used to be an
atheist ; but, watching the progress of this war, and
seeing how all its events have worked together to
secure the freedom of all men, I have become con-

vinced there is a Great Intelligence that governs the
universe, and has this country in his especial keeping." I never doubted this great truth ; but a knowledge of the inside history of some of the pivotal
events of this war has brought it home to me with
a vividness that has made me at times fancy I could
see the hand of God leading this people through
the Red Sea of battle to a promised land of lasting
peace and prosperity. And, my young reader, if you
reflect on my imperfect narrative of the discovery
and suppression of this great conspiracy, if you notice
the singular manner in which the right fact was disclosed at precisely the right time, and how wonderfully each actor in the drama was adapted to the very
part he had to perform, I think you too will be convinced that One, whose wisdom is past all finding
out, rules "in the armies of heaven and among the
inhabitants of the earth."

THE END.

Cambridge : Stereotyped and Printed by Welch, Bigelow, & Co.

Resolved that
I like this book very much and
I shall keep it very long. I have
never heard of Mr. Edmund Who
before but I am sure he writes
good books if all of his books are as
good as that. I have finished every
story but sometime shall read
it over.   John Philip Troxell.

Resolved — that I never liked
a book better in my life.
I shall prize it always.
In my other "resolved"
I said every story. Now
I intend to read it again
I hope I shall like it again
                    John Philip Sirois
5/26/1909/ 6. P.m